Sweet as Cane

Sweet as Cane

by Stephanie McCoy

Pen & Mouse Books
Berkeley

Pen & Mouse Books
7523 Fairmont Avenue
El Cerrito, CA 94530

An imprint of Saturday Morning and a Slow Rain Press

Grateful acknowlegment is made to Duke University Press for permission to reprint the following:
"Lullabye," in The Frank C. Brown Collection of North Carolina Folklore, Frank C. Brown, pp. 184-184. Copyright, 1952. Duke University Press. All rights reserved. Reprinted with permission from the publisher. "A saying," in The Frank C. Brown Collection of North Carolina Folklore, Frank C. Brown, pp. 592-592. Copyright, 1952. Duke University Press. All rights reserved. Reprinted with permission from the publisher.

PUBLISHERS-CATALOGING-IN-PUBLICATION DATA
McCoy, Stephanie
Sweet as Cane: a novel/Stephanie McCoy
p. cm
1. Women photographers. 2. Folklore—North Carolina. 3. Lullabies.
4. American Literature—Southern States. 5. Death
PS3613.C38576.S94 2010
813.54-dc22

Cover photo courtesy of the Graham Pilecki Collection
Printed and bound in the United States of America
FIRST EDITION
1 3 5 7 9 10 8 6 4 2

ISBN-13: 9780976236276

For
Jane Brooks & Ella Jane

Ask not my story,
Lest you hear at length
Of sorrows where sweet hope
Has lost its way.

—Julia Cameron, "On a Portrait," 1875

Cast of Characters

Cane Walker, town photographer, infant post-mortem specialist
Darleen Walker, Cane's mother and town mortician

Mrs. Grace Haydon
Mr. Rolland Haydon, her husband
Mercy Haydon, their older daughter
Lily Haydon, their youngest daughter

Mr. Benjamin Ladder, Grace Haydon's childhood friend
Mrs. Ina Ladder, his wife

Mr. Riley Trunk
Mrs. Rachel Trunk, his wife
Ulla Trunk, their daughter and Mercy Haydon's friend

Mr. Lyon
Mrs. Lyon, his wife, but called Miss Dunnet by all in town
King Lyon, their son
Eunice, King's cousin
Jack Pliney, family gardener
Minish, child of worker living on Lyon property
Nellie, child of worker living on Lyon property

Dewey "Winkie Jr." Lamm, a local young man
Mr. "Winkie Sr." Lamm, his father
Mrs. Lamm, his mother

The Cuffee Sisters: Tullah, Eullah and Buellah, sage ladies

Granny Ma'am, country doctor

Mr. Kincaid, traveling salesman

Reverend Mitchell, minister

Dr. Knox, visiting Northerner

Mitty Hyde, neighbor

Mrs. Sunn, town gossip-keeper

Marrow, North Carolina
October 1957

Black & White

"Joe Monroe cut off his toe
And hung it up to dry;
All the girls began to laugh
And Joe began to cry."

Cane Walker sang the lullaby to her subject. *Click.*
The pulse light made the baby shine like a glow-bug. Cane was careful not to disturb the Irish linen christening dress with the silk lace trim. She already had one of those in her collection. But the silver locket with the dogwood design on the front and a tobacco leaf engraved on the backside had just the right weight. She lifted it off Baby Dunnet, but it caught on the neck of the gown. Dang, if Miss Dunnet hadn't pinned it to the collar. The child remained steady. Cane hated it when her subjects and the setting she had created were disturbed — even by her own hand.

Click. She thought she should have at least one photograph of herself in the act of thievery; even so, she turned her face away from the camera. Her doctor's coat, which she wore to look professional, hung loose. Her long, muddy-brown hair and thin, poised fingers were in full view. Small hands and skinny fingers were needed for her kind of work. It was easier to grasp a reedy neck or scoop up a powdered bottom.

The silver oval fell into her pocket and clinked against the knife she'd taken from Ulla Trunk's father the night before. Ulla's father had large hands and sausage fingers that had been in the sun too long. At the moons of his fingernails he had shoots of tough black hairs sticking out like wires. He'd scraped the insides of her sinner box after he'd jumped on top of her. She wished she had been photographing Mr. Trunk's body. Her foot still ached from kicking him.

Later she would add the new items to her case of antiques and whatnots from her clients.

Click. Baby Dunnet had eaten those red chirp-berries, but he probably would have died anyway. Cane had been hard-pressed to get the stain out of the child's three pointed teeth. Baby teeth were so pure and easy to remove, though she let these ones stay since they had a religious look about them: Father, Son, Holy Ghost. She had used a bit of cleanser on a tiny Q-Tip that the dermatologist from Raleigh had given her to swab the pus bumps that flared up on her own face now and then.

Click.

Cane's mother, Darleen Walker, had done a good job of preparing the body, except for the teeth. Darleen, the only mortician in the greater Marrow area, owned the Sweet Hereafter Funeral Home. Cane's mother always did the babies up right. A bit overdone Cane thought, but the parents were weepy-pleased, saying their children looked better now than they had when they were alive.

Cane's side of the business was brisk. It seemed like more babies were dying than living, but the doctor said it wasn't half as bad as the Spanish Influenza of 1918. Cane never did understand why people wanted to show off photographs of their misfortune. Most of her customers set her photographs out for special occasions with their best china. She kept copies of her work in an album, but she didn't parade them around like circus curiosities.

Miss Dunnet's odds so far had been in favor of death. In fact, they say she died a little bit herself when she married Henry

Lyon, so most folks still called her by her maiden name, as if to keep her alive. Cane had photographed two other Dunnet babies. She figured this would be the last attempt, since Miss Dunnet was no longer a Georgia peach and a live one squeezed out between the first and second deaths. A little boy Miss Dunnet named King.

Cane had once years ago told another customer, Mr. Benjamin Ladder, that he shouldn't breed ever again. He was grieving too hard to notice her impertinence. She had just repeated to him what her mother and some of the other folks in town had told her, not even in a whisper. But when Cane heard the sound of her words fall out of her mouth and crack on the floor, she felt sad for him. His first child was blue, so blue that the only thing Cane would take from the infant catafalque where the baby lay was a letter Mr. Ladder had written to his son. And the folded note wasn't touching the child's skin. She was sure that baby was still a little bit alive. The expression on his face kept changing, even when she asked her mother to set his mouth. Mr. Ladder's baby was trying to tell her something she didn't want to hear. But that was long ago, when she had just started working next door to her mother. She had been too young to draw a paycheck, but her mother had gotten the former photographer to sign-on Cane as an apprentice.

Click. The Dunnet child was all done. Cane lifted it off the black velvet cloth attached to the backboard of the portable display case. She paused a moment and rocked it back and forth, singing softly before she slipped it into the applewood coffin Miss Dunnet's brother had made special for the occasion.

Cane shoved the casket with her good foot through the adjoining room to her mother's place of business. She wondered if the bridal-wreath bath she took late last night had reconnected her inner skin.

Betsey Sunn Speaks Her Mind
(1940)

*O*n the day of Grace's wedding, you could see the foreign smile, like fractured porcelain, on her face. Her dress was armored with five layers of silk and edged with antique black lace she had sewed on herself. She had ordered it from a mail-away special she'd noticed in Life magazine. She claimed it was the 'something old' portion of her outfit. Grace Pearl was too smart for the likes of Marrow, and some might say she had been born out of her time, not ahead or behind, just not at the right time for who she was. Grace was at war with herself, for being caught, is what I'd say, or caught by the wrong man.

Rolland Haydon's mother collected dolls, the fancy kind you had to order from Europe. People say Grace was supposed to be a life-size version for Rolland's mother, but it didn't work out that way.

And Rolland Haydon, bless his kind soul, didn't show a hint of insight about his wife. Though he wasn't from Marrow, he was from the Piedmont area and some folks insisted that counted for more than it should. Seemed like if a suitor came from out of the area he was a stranger, even if he was from North Carolina. It's funny how everyone wants to be so pure and yet we are all mixed. They say the blood of the Paw Creek Indians is in all of us whether we like it or not. They say whites and coloreds are all from one batter, too.

But the mixture of Rolland and Grace didn't fold-in well. Though just a week before the nuptials, at the Firefly Festival, it was so dark out you couldn't tell one skin color from another, one sex from

5

the other, one partner from another. Everybody and critter looked the same, except for a few honored glowbugs that pierced the sky like jagged pie-pricks.

Those folks who did have their eyes in order could have seen the way Ben Ladder gazed at Grace, as if he'd lost something he'd thought he'd always have.

If you had been looking by the courthouse where the trees once grew, you would have seen Cane Walker wearing a white mask. The one her mother made her put on, even when she went out at night. Her amber eyes were as bright as the bugs she was trying to snap up.

Aside from that, the big talk these days is about the volcanic movements in His Glory Cemetery. Just down Cardinal Street on your way out of town. The older graves rise up after a severe storm, and seem to be in protest over what is taking place in Marrow, in the whole County. In the colored and potters' sections the unmarked graves and even the marked ones have been shifting for years. It could be the ghosts of the dead babies the pearly girls didn't want their families to know about, or perhaps it's the small circus buried in the eastern corner of His Glory, where occasionally a decaying carousel horse emerges with its mouth open and its one remaining glass eye catches the light of the sun or moon.

No one seems to know about that for sure. Yet, I do know that Grace Haydon got married and that should account for something, rumors aside.

At the Edge of the Crying Water
(Cane)

The shortcut from the cemetery to the Tear River is easy but dark. I sometimes travel three or four times a night between the two. They are my real homes. Jack Pliney says Tear River water, as muddy as it is, has cleansing powers that the Paw Creek Indians used for medicinal purposes. Jack Pliney collects samples from the river, but I never have seen anyone drink it. After I've been crying, I come here and dip my hand into the river and rub my face with the water. Maybe it will help. Jack Pliney says his ancestors' blood is what made it change from mirror-like to murky.

I don't believe him for sure, but he told me that after the British invaded this area way back in 1700, most of the Paw Indians disappeared by choice. The Paw had a spring ritual of cutting open a pregnant doe and cooking her baby, still in the birthing sack. This was a part of their offering to the land they lived on, to their God. The soldiers didn't care for that kind of religion, so they killed the Indians when they could catch them.

I'm sitting at the river now. The dogwood and sourwood trees hang above me and keep the eater-bugs busy. My feet push at the edge of the river. I come here and think about what this river was like when it was free running with the whippoorwills, turtle doves, and the bobwhites calling, with sparkling trout and horny pikes rippling the river water, the smell of wet clay rising like thick steam. The dangerous sections, with fallen tree limbs and roots for miles high and wide, are really the spirits of the Paw Creek Indians, I am convinced. Jack Pliney said they disappeared by cutting open their bellies. They walked to the center of the river and let the water cleanse their bodies of blood. That was better than letting the British go after them. When their insides were empty, their bodies wound around each other, like coils of dirt, and slowly submerged.

They named it the Tear River, not for the Paw, but for all the whites and coloreds that get caught in the river and can't escape. The tears of their friends and relatives helpless on the red clay banks are why they named the river what they did.

I still dig around for Indian relics some nights, but try not to take too many things. It's bad luck.

I often see shadows coming from the water, but I'm not scared. I sing lullabies to them, like,

> *Baby, baby, hush-a-bye,*
> *Must you be awake now?*
> *Sweet my lamb, come close your eye,*
> *Sleep for mother's sake now.*

If that doesn't satisfy them, my face usually scares the shadows that turn out to be people. My mother told me I should try and find some hope, something in me that other people would admire. At the end of the day, in the cemetery where I sing to the children, or by this river, my face is my guardian, a kind of armor, like the caul that almost strangled me at birth, and then settled on my face and rotted the skin.

When I was a child, my mother would look at me, at nighttime, after avoiding my face all day. She would hold me and rock me back and forth and sing the songs and charms that her colored maid had sung to her as a child. My favorite charm was *Firebug, Firebug, fly away home, Your house is on fire and now you're all alone.*

After Mama's brothers died, Mama's mother, Grandma Winnie, took to her bed and Mama was left to the cooks and servants. It took 30 years of nurses before Grandma Winnie choked to death on watermelon rind pickles. It was a blessing. In her will, the one thing she left me was a bolt of indigo and white plaid fabric.

Jack Pliney says the Paw Indians were geniuses because they could live off the land around them. They counted their corn by the number of hills that were planted. That was keen smart. These days there aren't many hills left in this area. The topography of the area has been altered. Until the invaders came to North Carolina, the Paw Creek Indians lived calmly and their babies thrived. I guess they would call me an invader, too.

Kick-the-Can
(1950)

*M*ercy, Ulla, Minish, Nellie, and Eunice, King Lyon's rich cousin from Raleigh, would visit His Glory Cemetery late in the day to play. No boys were allowed because they always cheated or knocked off an angel wing from a gravestone. The girls played kick-the-can between the markers and only had trouble if there was a new grave nearby and the can would sometimes lodge itself into the new mound of dirt, especially if an afternoon shower had passed through.

They played at dusk, when neither color nor money had anything to do with winning. Though Eunice kept reminding the others of her wealth and she complained that Nellie and Minish had an advantage because of their dark skins, the girls played together in unison like a tiny rebel army. Mercy and Ulla had been coming to the cemetery since they were five years old. They knew the layout blindfolded and spun around.

Today, Mercy had raced over into one of the older sections of the cemetery. As she went to hide, she was startled by a soft sound, someone singing a mother's song. Mercy stumbled on a large grave marker. The family name was Dunnet and the letters were wider and deeper than the others. As she ran behind it, she fell over a woman who was kneeling at a smaller grave behind the Kent slab.

"Ma'am, I'm sorry. I didn't see you."

"My name's not Ma'am, Mercy Haydon," the woman said without looking up. Mercy wanted to run away, but curiosity kept her rigid. The woman's muddy brown hair covered her face and she wore a large coat. Mercy couldn't decipher a thing.

"How do you know my name?" she asked with a defiance that was growing as quick as her eight-year-old body. Her short page-boy cut gave her confidence, even though she hated the red streaks in her hair. They came from her father's side of the family, or that is what her mother had always told her.

"Everyone knows about the Haydons." As the woman said this, she peered up at Mercy and Mercy saw a face with pulled-back skin, covered with rock-like bumps. Staring at the woman, Mercy pinched her finger to steady herself. God works in mysterious ways. That's what her father would say during uncomfortable moments. In that flash, while the two of them gazed at one another, Mercy figured it out.

"You're Cane Walker, aren't you? You never go out during the day?" Mercy asked, collecting courage and speed with her insight. She waited and Cane didn't utter a sound. "Your mama's the mortician and you help her clean and wash and touch all the dead bodies in town."

"No," Cane said, biting down on a small pebble, as if she were in pain. "I'm a portrait photographer." As she said this, Eunice, Ulla, Minish, and Nellie came running up. They froze as Cane's face came into their view. They halted so quickly that they put out their hands for protection and for a moment they all held each other as if connected.

Cane spat out the pebble, got up, and started to leave. Mercy knew from her mother that Cane never said much or stayed in the vicinity for long. Most folks who had seen Cane had only set eyes on her because they wanted a portrait taken. She was the youngest photographer in town and the only one around willing to photograph dead babies. Mr. Holt's photography studio handled public events like weddings, parades, and school functions, but he was just getting by, holding onto his health by a mattress spring. People came from other counties and as far away as Wilmington to do business with Cane. Mercy had asked her mother why Cane was so good at taking pictures of dead people. Her mother just shook her head and said Cane sees what other people don't.

Mercy's friends stood as silent as the stone markers. They tried to look smaller, but their bulging eyes betrayed their awareness of how facial features consume people first. Nellie and Minish spoke in finger codes that Mercy was still learning how to decipher. Cane watched them, too, and seemed to know their stubby, digit language. She lifted her hand as if she was going to say something, but changed her mind. Her coat billowed out with the evening wind and her buttons tapped at a stone marker.

As Cane headed toward the gates of the cemetery, Eunice shouted after her, "Hey, let's play Grunt, Ugly Pig, Grunt."

Mercy went over and hit Eunice, and Eunice hit both Nellie and Minish. Ulla was hiding behind Eunice and escaped attack since she had learned long ago how to avoid it. Then they all fell into a swarm of laughter, poking at one another and momentarily forgetting what had caused it.

Mercy halted and looked in Cane's direction, and saw Cane had stopped. She stared at Mercy with her marble eyes that were hardly held in lids. It looked like Cane had no eyelashes. Mercy saw a glistening on the sides of her face one would call cheeks. Mercy couldn't tell if it was medicine-lotion, tears, or hate.

"Eunice, she'll never forget that," Mercy said. "Cane Walker remembers everything that has ever been done to her."

"Oh, who cares about that johnny-house face? King says all she does most days is take snapshots of dead babies. She probably wishes she had a live one for herself." Eunice stopped and lowered her voice. "All the love powder in Raleigh couldn't help her. I bet those nuns near Asheville wouldn't take her in." Eunice let a deep breath go and caught their eyes with her God-given authority. "Even Jesus would say no to a bride like Cane."

Mercy had no idea what Eunice meant, but the severity of what she said made them all bow their heads.

It was suppertime and the mothers in the neighborhood could be heard calling their children. The Lyon's servant rang a bell. Grace Haydon had the softest yell in Marrow. It carried through the trees as *if it knew how to find the designated person, as if her call could echo in your heart.*

Ulla's mother was dead and her father rarely expected her home much. Ulla would go with Mercy, while Nella and Minish would follow Eunice to the Lyon household, where Eunice lived when it suited her mother. Nellie and Minish grew up on the Lyon property with their parents. They lived in garden sheds that had come directly from the Sears catalog. Their houses shimmered at night like torches.

"Wait for me, little niggras," Eunice said. She grabbed at their clothes. Nella and Minish stopped and didn't say anything except with their fingers. They had walked with Eunice many times before.

"Eunice, I keep telling you, you should say Negro or nothing at all," Mercy said. Eunice picked at her eyelashes. Mercy peered at the gates of the cemetery, trying to figure out how Cane knew about her family, just by her voice. So many people in town knew more than she did. Even Ulla had secrets she didn't share.

"Yeah, says who?" Eunice answered as she linked arms with Nellie and Minish and skipped out of the cemetery.

Before leaving, Ulla and Mercy put their hands on their thighs and then clapped them together and then against each other's palms.

"Miss Mary Mack, Mack, Mack
All dressed in black, black, black
With silver buttons, buttons, buttons,
All down her back, back, back."

They continued through the rest of the verses, slapping their limbs until they stung.

A Photographer in the Making

At six in the morning, before the inhabitants of Marrow had woken up for the day, Cane arrived at work. The one-story clapboard building was connected, like an afterthought, to her mother's two-story mortuary, the second floor of which contained coffins propped up at the windows for customers to see and file cabinets of records behind them. By law Darleen Walker had to keep the records, otherwise she would have tossed them into the backyard like she did with the love notes and other mementos people left for their deceased relatives.

The photography studio was located just off the town square, set back from the street, away from the light of day. Cane turned a key in the lock; though most people in town kept their doors unlocked, she did not.

The smell of D-76, stop-bath, and fixer, her daily ointments, permeated the room. She switched on a small Tiffany lamp with the amber bulb that shed just enough light for her to see around. She took the cover off her 8x10 view camera and loaded the Plus X film in the holders for the day.

A woman from Durham had made an appointment for herself and her dead daughter for later that morning. She had wanted to know if Cane would photograph the two of them lying down, and then sitting up like two daguerreotypes the woman had seen from her grandmother's collection. Cane was obliging; requests like that hadn't bothered her for years.

Cane set up the two scenes. She smoothed out the velvet

on the formal sitting chair and adjusted the painted weeping willow and duck pond backdrop. She lit a few tall candles and checked and rechecked the pulse lights. On the bed where her clients would lie she sprinkled orange water, and she placed vases of roses, leftovers from her mother's shop, around the bed, which had belonged to the studio's previous owner. Though she kept the four front windows covered, there was a tear in the side window curtain, and the October rays slipped inside.

When Cane had seen light as a child, she thought she could hold onto it by hugging it. She wrapped her arms around the rays and ended up clutching herself, rocking back and forth. She would stare at the light and when it reflected colors she'd try to gather them up, to put them in order.

Early on she had learned that light shining on her face was as bad as telling the truth after a lie. When her mother had taken her outside shopping or around town, she would put a white cloth mask on Cane's face. Her mother had told her it would shield her from the sun, but Cane had discovered very abruptly it was to shield her from the reactions of others, if they had seen her disfigurement.

Her mother could make dead bodies complete, physically whole again, but Cane was the reminder to her mother of what was alive, unfixable. In Marrow, they say blood is thicker than mud, but at times Cane felt closer to the mud, especially the rich soil near the banks of the Tear River and the pliable dirt at the cemetery.

Cane walked into the developing room at the back. Her latest work was hanging on the drying line. The three porcelain developing trays sat on a table next to the wall that connected her with her mother's business. She could barely see in this room. The muted light from the stained glass lamp in the front kept her from tripping.

She had usually found comfort in the dark. Fireflies were the only exception and she captured them in jelly jars. She had carried them inside and used them to illuminate her bedroom. She played with the shadows she made with her fingers against the wall and with a carousel horse eye that she kept by her bedside table.

Cane had put that eye up to the insect light and saw the fractures inside, saw how on some nights the thick amber glass would reflect nothing, but other nights there would be colors shooting out like spears.

To keep Cane occupied at home and inside as she got older, Cane's mother brought her a deluxe Brownie Box camera she'd bartered for with a couple who couldn't afford a funeral for their child. After the first roll of film came out blank, Darleen let Cane light up her room with candles and extra funeral lamps so that the pictures would be properly exposed and develop completely.

Cane created scenes in her room: A porcelain dolly in a baby cradle. A birthday party for herself. She dragged the hall table into her room and covered it with a pink linen tablecloth and five napkins. Ten years old, she coveted living friends, even one.

Darleen Walker had taken her mask-covered daughter to work with her ever since Cane had come home from the hospital. Sometimes Darleen had had to go over to the cemetery and Cane always went with her. As Cane got older, she had surreptitiously started collecting objects from the dead people, to make her photographs more interesting. The first thing she had stolen were baby teeth, since they were so easy to remove. It made her nervous if she thought about it too much, though she didn't need to worry; Darleen had been stealing trinkets from the plots for as long as she could remember and didn't give a hoot about what Cane did, or what other people said or saw.

Cane had also collected strands of deceased children's hair and she pasted them on cardboard rounds. Then she'd draw the kind of face she wished she'd been born with. She'd set up a family of five around her and then take a photograph. Pretending they lived a busy life, she would make them grow up, get married, have babies, and then die. Cane carefully set up each stage of their lives and then used her mother's tools — the coffins, the make-up, the drapes, the flowers — to create each person's death, whenever it seemed right.

When old man Tatter died, he left his photography shop and equipment to Darleen in payment for a spectacular funeral. Darleen insisted Cane help her with his sunken body that smelled like a mixture of chemicals and moldy turnips. Darleen made her change his clothes, fix his pockmarked face, and take his picture. With the help of Mr. Tatter's Kodak manuals and the time she had apprenticed with him, Cane developed the film and printed it.

Cane's mother had gotten it into her head that Cane would be able to make a living as a portrait photographer. She instructed Cane to put the overexposed post-mortem in the window of the old shop to advertise her new business. Cane didn't have much to say about it, but she liked working in the dark. And as it turned out, she usually worked with dead bodies, so she didn't have to respond to the look of horror most folks felt as they gazed across her raw-looking skin with its jagged markings like the inside of a crater.

Cane pulled the portraits from the drying line. The chill of the upcoming holidays made her shiver, although Halloween had to be the worst. It opened the door to unkindness every year. But Cane didn't fancy any holiday or event gathering.

Last week, three girls from across the Tear River had come by for their sweet-sixteen shots. Mr. Holt was all booked up and they couldn't wait. The girls were wearing their frilly whites and Mary Jane's. Their cheeks were clear and their eye lashes long. Cane had hidden her face behind the camera just as they had come into her shop. She had it all set up, so they wouldn't have much of a chance to see her. Cane had celebrated her 16th birthday by reading a magazine and eating lemon pound cake her mother had bought day old at the bakery.

But now she could look at the girls with her full face. She'd taken fifteen individual portraits and five group shots. She carried the best individual pictures and went into the front room. From the wooden desk she used for billing and customer files, she pulled out a large oval mirror with a beaded handle and moved the lamp closer to her skin.

With make-up from her mother's shop, she carefully compared the pictures to her face. She painted her sparse albino lashes black, dipped the brushes in the apricot-hued powder, in flat jars full of red, purple, and orange paints, and tried to make her face into the beauties she had photographed.

The doorbell rang. The woman from Durham stepped inside the shop carrying the child like it was alive.

"We're here now, baby," the woman said. "I'm Mrs. Gibbs and this is Baby Ireni." She removed her coat and patted down the white satin dress she was wearing. With Cane's permission she went over to the bed and lay down with her baby. The woman didn't notice Cane's colored face. She seemed entranced by her dead child.

Cane was flustered behind the mask of make-up. She fumbled with her camera. As the woman closed her eyes, she held the dead girl tightly. Cane went over to the child and put a bunch of violets in the child's hand. She had to unclench Baby Ireni's fingers. A tear ran down from the mother's eye, and Baby Ireni's mouth opened as if she had seen Cane Walker's face for the first time.

House of Dehydration
(Mercy 1950)

I was wide-awake when the nightmare passed through our home. I couldn't not follow it around. I noticed, because it was summer and the nights were rarely dark, that the light bulbs in parts of the house had been broken. I checked each room stepping on crystal points of glass. In the bathroom I got double-jabbed because there were two ceiling lights.

From the top of the stairs I saw my father sitting in a highchair in the front parlor. I tiptoed down 10 wooden steps. At each board I took a new breath.

I asked him: Do you know me?

His cardboard mouth said: We come from a place called Dehydration.

Blood dribbled out between my toes. I tapped my feet back and forth to "Yes sir, that's my baby," making a ruby necklace around me.

The next evening, my mother left for the hospital and I was sent to the Ladders' house next door. I got to sleep in their sunroom, with the screens surrounding me like a butterfly net, a thick breeze swaying me to sleep. As was my habit, I got up around 3 a.m. to get a glass of water. I'd known the Ladders my entire life and their house was as familiar to me as my mother's pocketbook. I soft-heeled myself into the living room and saw a light already on in the kitchen. Mr. Ben Ladder was sitting at the table, his hands cupped over his eyebrows. Tears dribbled down his face, making streaks like tiny streams that disappeared.

Stinky heat moved all over his body. His morning shower was a few hours away along with the Spicy Talc he used. Every dad on our block used Spicy Talc, but Mr. Ladder needed it the most. Our bathrooms were neck and neck, so I knew from experience that daily he carefully shook out a molehill of powder and rubbed it twice over his upstairs and downstairs parts.

He wore only white, crumpled underwear that were too long; they almost came to his knees.

I could see a bit of his pee-paw. Gulping on a cry-laugh, he said my mother's name.

Thirst kept tickling me the rest of the night.

My sister Lily was born the following morning. They had to cut my mother from her rib cage to below her belly to get Lily out.

My mother has a shiny pink line now down her stomach. Sometimes when she is worried she takes her pinkie finger and traces the line, up and down, up and down.

Truth Be Told
(Mercy)

My God-given name, or the one my mother picked out of the Bible by closing her slate-green eyes, dropping the Revised Standard Version on the floor, and groping around until she found the open book, was Mercy. The rest of it was Palmer Haydon. I have brown eyes and brown hair that turns bronze in the summer. At every checkup the doctor says my weight and my height are average, as if that were a compliment.

My mother had a baby with Ben Ladder. I wasn't even born yet. But I'm sure it's true. I asked Jack Pliney once since he knows all about plants and dirt and he just looked the other way. But Darleen Walker told me about it by mistake, or so she said later. She owns the Sweet Hereafter Mortuary in town and guzzles bootlegged Scuppernong wine at tea time, tea time being whenever it suits her. But you can't call her a drunkard. Darleen Walker always keeps herself ready for the next customer.

I walked into her mortuary one day, requesting donations for our school raffle. I had prepared all week for asking for prizes, standing in front of a sheet of foil so I could see myself. My mother won't keep mirrors in the house. She says they make you grow older than you really are and once she broke one. She didn't want to court any more bad luck. So my sister Lily held onto a large piece of the screechy stuff and I worked myself into a decent presentation.

I had heard Darleen Walker had extra sets of teeth that she

kept in the empty coffins, just to scare you into buying, I guess. But the day I went to see her, she was full of fermented juice, which she always referred to as her Chinaman. She had all her sets of teeth lined up.

"Good morning, troops!" she said to them before turning to me.

"Mercy Haydon! I didn't hear of another death in your family," she said as she bobbed her head in my direction. "Poor little Baby Miles."

The door had a chime on it that made off-key sounds. I looked down into the coffins; there were so many around, one could hardly see the floor. The room smelled of fresh-cut cedar.

"Miss Walker, I —" Her breath replaced the air in the room and made me sick. "Everyone in my family is fine. I'm here as a representative of the Brunswick High School Raffle Committee." She turned away and I thought she hadn't heard me, or that she was sipping some more of her afternoon brew.

"I can show you a picture of him. Your mother's mistake. So blue. So blue. A river of veins. Cane did a good job with this one. It was her first infant portrait." She'd pulled open a file cabinet. "She cried when she saw the limp thing, but your mother had brought the prettiest baby gown I had ever seen. The little one looked so alive. The embroidery was as good as Ina Ladder's. See, Mercy, here it is."

The black-and-white photograph had a strange hue. The child was blue and the color pierced the paper like God had left his mark.

"A photographer from Greensboro told me he thought for sure Cane had tampered with the photograph, but your older brother's spirit was just in transition from death to dust," Darleen said.

The outfit dangled from the child's limbs and was blurry as if it had been in motion.

"Miss Walker, we don't have a baby," I dug my pinkie into my neck. "I'm the oldest."

"Of course you are," Darleen said. "Now. Some people find comfort in these death portraits during their time of grieving. Dead babies are always the saddest. Just ask Mr. Ladder. Their homes to carry them to heaven or hell are so tiny."

I started to leave her business with a scream like an ice shard piercing my throat. What did Daddy know? I am the oldest, I said to myself. I am the oldest. As I headed towards the doorway, I heard her say,

"Fret not yourself, Mercy, it tends only evil. So blue, so blue, so blue." Her voice trailed off. "Chinaman, where did you get to?" Before I could get out of earshot, she sang what sounded like a strange lullaby to nobody I had seen.

> *"It's what did you have for supper, Bucky, my sweet, my one? Oh, what did you have for supper, my own, my one?"*

I took myself off of the Raffle Committee. I said I had too much homework to do. Miss Walker sent in a 10-dollar gift certificate toward funeral expenses as a donation. Three weeks later, I heard she had checked herself into the Tear River Presbyterian Home for a temporary visit. Rumor had it that she often checked herself into the Home to see who was coming her way soon.

I tried to follow her daughter Cane around town. She was Miss Walker's only child. Who and where her father was, nobody seemed to know. Cane hogged information too, but I thought I could get something out of her, especially if she didn't know I was listening.

Betsey Sunn, who lived across the street from us, said that when Cane was born her face was so disfigured that they turned down the lights in nursery. She has all the right features; they just are mixed up and mashed together like a child's finger painting. It runs in her family, they say. And she some-times pulls at her face, so she has scabs. I knew she took photo-graphs at the shop next door to her mother's mortuary. If you wandered inside, she rarely showed her face from behind the camera. She's 23 now, but she looks 100. I'm 15, but I look 21.

The only time I've ever seen her full of face was at the cemetery once, years ago. She never goes around town in the daylight, even if we're suffering from summer silence, when the air is so thick it stops and you hear yourself breathe and everybody else, but you feel like dying, 'cause the air is full of other people's leftovers.

Cane lives in the dark, even between afternoon storms. She has no friends, not even one. Cane couldn't buy a friend. My mother is her own best friend, but that's not the same.

Thundershowers pass by Marrow daily, not just in the summertime. My mother, Grace, calls them circles of death. I like them because they were about the only thing you could rely on. Even death itself wasn't a sure bet. Milton Patton told Daddy he read about a pill Duke University was developing that would make you live forever. And of course, you could freeze yourself and have someone shoot you into space like the Communists were doing.

I'd rather die of the white death or the black one. You could get either of them whether you were Negro or white, by just being next to someone, breathing their bacteria-infested, odor-filled germs. We learned about the history of plagues and diseases in Mrs. Hanks' Health Education class. When I told my parents about these diabolical conditions in detail at dinner, they both looked at each other and Daddy put another huge spoonful of chow-chow on his plate. I told them I was sure Cane Walker had a secret disease, an ungodly one. Though I knew it wasn't true, I told them Cane was really named for Cain from the Bible just to see what they would do. Miss Sunn had told me Darleen named her Cane so people would think sweet things before they looked at her straight on.

My mother just said, "Mercy," like she said about most things.

Late October Harvest

"Swines do best in this state, even better than the mighty tobacco and our prized cotton. They breed on infection, disease, bacteria, and pestilence and turn out the tastiest ham in the region. My secret fertilizer of poudrette works wonders for my crops, too," Riley Trunk said on the steps to a crowd that wasn't there. "I put up country ham and sausages in chitlin' jackets like you've never tasted. During pig scalding, I make the colored boys do it just to remind them where they stand. My grandpappy had 200 cattle at one time and just as many slaves. The cattle had more value, just like today."

The only other person on the porch of Tillie's Grocery & Feed, Henry Lyon, looked up in amazement, part of an apple lodged in the corner of his mouth like a pipe. "You mean to tell me, Riley, that you are still using —" Henry looked around him and lowered his voice "— using night soil to tend your land?"

Worried that Henry Lyon's attention might wander, Riley nodded and continued, "Say, did you hear of that wedding up north where a colored boy stood in for the father of the white girl? Said he was in the Army, probably the Salvation Army shelter." Riley laughed so hard, he almost retched.

"Wasn't even a clean wedding."

Henry Lyon shook his head, and put the *Daily Gazette* closer to his face as he tried to locate the latest price for tobacco like he did every morning, except Sundays. He made a suck-suck-slurp sound on the apple core hanging from his lips. To anyone who knew him this was a sign to leave him alone.

Riley retreated into the store and bought a few items and left, careful not to disturb Mr. Henry Lyon.

Riley needed to get back to harvesting the watermelons he had planted by the river. There was talk of river thieves returning, and he wanted to be sure he had harvested before he shot at any trespassers. He'd hate for the melons to get damaged. He already had an overripe batch he wanted Ulla to cook up into syrup. But he was pleased that he had made an impression on Henry Lyon. The richest man in town and they had talked at length that very day.

The only books Riley Trunk owned were the almanacs. They were holier than the Bible. His family had used them since 1828. He had all the years stacked up neatly in the sitting room of his farmhouse, with 1957 splayed open. Next to the magazines were cans of tobacco from the Taylor Brothers in Winston-Salem. He chewed Red Coon Tobacco variety and would toss the empty cans into the sky and shoot at them. Since his dead-eye-gunner reputation was at stake every time he took aim, he was careful to make the shot hit its mark. That's why he kept away from drinking. Steady hands made him a winner. Winkie Sr. had been state champion as a youth, but Riley doubted he could even shoot at one of his customers in his soda shop in Marrow. No, the best shooters were the county boys from the Skeeter Grove area. Rumor had it they used each other as target practice. Still, Riley had won the rifle event at the Harvest Fair last year, but he knew he needed to keep at it and was kind of hoping those river thieves would show up.

With the help of the almanac, his best crops this year were beans and corn. Tobacco had worn out its welcome on his land. It was yellow or all black and the bud tips hooked downward as if gasping for air. And the cotton he grew had a blue hue to it this season. Buyers didn't want that. The bug powder he'd gotten from the state didn't help his crops, except he noticed it had kept away those clamoring morning birds and the rodents seemed to find their contentment elsewhere.

He'd planted grapevines right after Darleen Walker's mistake had startled him last week near the river. Cane had come to save the puppies. Imagine that female mess-up barging onto his land. She's lucky he didn't fill her up with buckshot. He had a right to do whatever he needed to do to the animals on his property. Hell, she touched dead babies all day. He had drowned his puppies according to the days of the week: Wednesday's child is full of woe, down another one goes. What was a few yappy pups to her? He told her she could photograph them all if she liked, right after he'd finished with them.

"They prettier than you, Cane Walker, alive or dead," Riley had told her. "Anyway, you're trespassing. It's not Halloween yet, scary-face! I'd shoot you dead, but I wouldn't want to waste a bullet."

Riley Trunk was well known in Marrow for firing off his gun and his opinions, but he particularly objected to Cane because her mother had spurned him years ago.

"It's bad enough that you beat your wife and own child," Cane had said, walking right up to his face. She'd heard that Riley was killing baby animals and it didn't settle right with her. She had to admit she didn't know what spirit had taken over her mind.

"You're a damn feisty one," Riley said. He grabbed her shoulder and shook her back and forth like she was one of Ulla's raggedy-dolls he used for target practice. He thought that would be enough to scare her off, but she took a swipe at him and horse-kicked him, so he shoved her away. She fell backwards, her elbows keeping part of her body above the dirt. Her billowy coat spread open like a fan. The accordion-skirt she was wearing flew up above her white panties. For a moment they both stopped and stared at her exposed skin. It was white, not porcelain, but chalky as if it hadn't ever seen the light of day.

Ever.

The wind was pulling at the blue cotton, but it wouldn't give.

Riley jumped on top of her and started moving around like he was squiggling in mud.

"I'll teach you never to come on to my property again."

Cane's mouth dropped open, but not a sound emerged. Riley's weight had taken her breath. There was a metal object in his shirt pocket that was digging at her chest. He ripped at her panties with one hand and tore them. He held her down with his other arm wedged at her neck.

A tear worked its way down the bumpy side of her face.

He used his shooting finger to scrape her insides in a rectangular motion.

Saliva collected in Cane's mouth, but her voice still failed her. Riley put the tip of his shooting finger to his lips and ran his tongue over it.

"Can't figure out why your Mama named you Cane. Pig innards taste sweeter than that."

Cane wrestled his arm free from her neck and managed to shove him sideways. He was done with her, so he let himself be moved. Cane grabbed the metal object, a pocketknife that had slipped out and rolled onto her feet.

"They say you do the same thing to Ulla." Cane spit in his direction. Riley stood up and leaned away. "That's why your wife killed herself!" Cane shouted. Some cotton flew off into the wind. Her nimble fingers helped her open the pocketknife and she charged at him one more time.

Riley froze. In fact he stayed right still as if lightning or death had seized him. He didn't know anyone had known the real cause of his wife's death. Hearing it spoken out loud had struck him dumb.

The rough blade slid easily into the side of his cheek. They stared at each other again. Cane twisted the knife to be sure she left a mark, yanked it out slow, and held the handle while Riley's blood spider-webbed on her arm.

Before she ran off she kicked him on in his kneecap, hurting her own foot in the process. The knife stuck to her palm, the blood working like sticky paste.

Riley winced, but his tongue pushed hard against the roof of his mouth.

He dropped into the dry red clay and felt the thick gash on his face. It burned from the slapping of the night air as he sat in his field. He grabbed a leaf of tobacco that the wind had dropped and chewed it into a pulp. Around him was a ring of bloodied cotton clusters. It had been a rough year for the farmers in Marrow County. Lots of crops were weak and diseased.

With his thumb he pushed the poultice into the wound. For a time he swayed back and forth, thinking. Blood spilled down his face marking up his clothes with lines that dribbled all the way to the earth but didn't sink in. He looked down at his hands.

Riley had worked the fields for so long his skin had changed from white to clay-color. He felt his cheek. The stubble on his face was thick and tar black. When he would lean down to talk to his daughter, Ulla, if he got too close she'd have tiny jabs on her skin where his facial hair had cut her. Damn scrawny thing. Couldn't whip a lick of farm sense into her.

He glanced over at the porch and caught Ulla staring at him while he cradled his body. She stared at him like he was crazy or foreign. She spent most of her time just staring. There was no hope for her. He was sorry his wife Rachel wasn't around, though she had extracted a promise from him on her dying bed that he wouldn't harm Ulla any more. The thought of her telling him what to do made him shake with anger. Still, he'd missed her more than once. Rachel had been smart about what crops to plant. She always wanted him to plant grapevines. Not just Scuppernong, but Isabella and Catawba. It was when she insisted on the Lincoln variety that they had had a fight over it. That pigeon-holed president. But he should have listened to Rachel. Wine was becoming popular, even if sometimes it had to be sold out of state or under the table. Why Henry Lyon's wife was selling it out her back door, he never understood. She had enough money to buy up the town, if she was ever straight enough to remember.

The Hunter's Moon pierced his fields highlighting the hue of his failing crops. Grapevines were the answer. The juiciest grapes in the county. He'd show her, though as he pondered the word he wasn't sure exactly which female he was referring to. They all got in the way of his progress.

Baking Tips from Mrs. Ladder
(1949)

"*D*id you know I lost one of my babies this morning, Mercy?" said Mrs. Ladder as she stepped out from behind her screen door. She was mixing a bowl of cake batter and as she walked to the edge of the porch, a bit of rain from the roof fell into the yellow bowl.

"I didn't know there were babies in your house, Mrs. Ladder." Mercy's thoughts froze like Eskimos Pies. She glanced at Mr. Ladder, who was shifting in a reedy, green rocker.

"Mrs. Ladder means that one of her mother rabbits has eaten one of her offspring like they do if one of them isn't right," he said to her slowly, as if he were able to whisper inside her mind, like she'd seen him do with her mother.

"About a year before you popped into the world, your mother helped a baby live; she located a wet-nurse for the motherless child," said Mrs. Ladder as she beat the batter to the rim.

"Of course, she wasn't one of our kind, though, was she, Mr. Ladder?"

"She was the salt of the earth, like all of us. Milk-fed." Mr. Ladder paused. "Faith is her name. You know her, Mercy; she's Jack Pliney's girl."

The batter spilled over the rim of the bowl and made a thud on the wooden porch. All eyes were on the wet mess as it spread out like a stain. *When one of them isn't right,* Mercy whispered to herself.

"You must be so excited about the new baby coming, Mercy," Mrs. Ladder said.

Mercy tapped her foot to a sound echoing in her heart. She bent over to the batter and wiped it off the porch with the cuff of her white, boat shirt.

"Sorry about the dead baby," Mercy said to the both of them and backed her way down the steps before she turned and ran home, stepping on every crack in the sidewalk.

A Doctor for Dirt
(Jack Pliney)

I don't care that the Haydon girls used to call me Mister Suh. It's not their fault they thought my name was Jack Suh, instead of Jack Pliney. Children learn by what they hear and see. All of us do.

I'm a gardener for a white man, Mr. Henry Lyon, but my aim in life is to be a botanist and a doctor to this land around me that is dying from earth decay. Not natural decay, but something that has etched itself into the land around here. Mama worries that Mr. Lyon might become angered by my inquiring ways. Her bloodline goes all the way back to the Paw Creek Indians, so she knows how unpredictable the white man can be. My father was a Negro and I take after him on the outside, but I'm more like my mother inside. Some days, though, the color of my skin changes just like the trees in autumn. Mama's convinced I'm becoming a part of the land. I do my job and educate myself at the same time.

When Mr. Lyon was throwing out a batch of books, I asked him if I could have them. The ones I use most are William Bartram's *Travels Through North and South Carolina* and John White's observations and paintings of early North Carolina. Mr. Lyon also threw away a batch of old almanacs and a leather Bible with passages of scripture torn out. The gold-stenciled name on the front said Ester Ray Dunnet. I asked him if it was OK to take Miss Dunnet's property and he said his wife wouldn't notice and that he'd ordered her a new one that had her married name on it anyway. I didn't need another Bible,

37

but there's something wrong with throwing one away even if it is damaged.

Right now I am trying to cure the diseased apple trees in Mr. Lyon's yard. They were neglected for years before I came on as gardener. Didn't Mr. Lyon know that when not kept up these fruit trees were breeding grounds for maggots, curculio, codling moth, cedar rust, and scab? Mr. Lyon was insistent on keeping them. His ancestors planted them and he was powerfully attached to the fruit they bore. It will take a few more months to get the infestation out of the orchard and the poison out of the dirt, at least on his property.

After my wife died, I became obsessed with the trouble in our soil. I was so worried that I sent my own daughter away. Faith lives out west now, with my cousin in California. She writes me often about the stagnant seasons and the mild-minded people that live there. But she is happy. I let her take the framed photograph that Cane Walker had taken of her mother and me. I have my memories, and Faith wanted the photograph so much.

Cane — that girl is an odd sort. I don't mean her face. Any of us could look like her on the outside, but it is underneath where there is or is not bounty of spirit. That's why the earth on top doesn't concern me. It is what lies beneath us that sets our future.

A long while back, Cane had brought over a photograph of another of Miss Dunnet's dead babies. After she had dropped it off, she wandered about the property and had come looking into our home. My wife and I were lucky to live on a patch of land set back from the Lyon home. Ages ago, our home was the chapel for the Lyon household. The Paw Creek meandered right near our doorway. I always told my wife we were protected by the yellow pines and live oaks surrounding us. That day Cane marched right inside, as I recall.

I didn't retreat from her like most folks do. We had seen

each other before on the banks of the Tear and at the cemetery. She'd sit in front of those tiny graves and sing.

We are both collectors. She collects to keep — in fact, stealing is a more accurate word — and I collect to study, to decipher what ails the land.

"How come your house is so narrow with those tall ceilings and colored windows?" Cane had said to me. Not in need of an answer, she continued poking around. She fingered a few of the books I had and felt the weight of a soapstone water jug that my wife's mother had given us.

"Where did this come from?" she said, holding it for longer than I would have liked.

"My wife's mother gave it to us on our wedding day. It had been passed down through the female line of the family, the surer kin." I had laughed, but Cane didn't know what to do with jokes.

We kept our place neat and clean, especially since it was once the Lord's house of worship. Cane had looked around our sparse household and took careful note of the walls. She ran her hands back and forth over the smooth surface. No cracks or chips in any of them. I got the feeling she didn't get invited into many homes in Marrow.

"Let me take a wedding picture for you. I need practice with live people. I'll give it to you for free. I make most of my money with the dead babies, but I need experience with newlyweds. You still have your clothes?"

I had nodded. I had wanted a picture of us together. My wife, Celie, had dreamed of a wedding photograph and had hoped that the child to come would have some remembrance of her parents' happy day.

"Can we come tomorrow? Sunday is our day off," I had responded, trying not to be too eager. At that time, and even now, when speaking to a white woman-child, I had to be careful.

Cane drops by regularly. She touches the bottles of dirt I collect and label from various regions of Marrow proper.

Yesterday when she left, Cane pointed to the glass specimens and smiled in her jigsaw way. "You're a thief like me, aren't you?"

The Warmth of Marble
(1920s)

race and Ben started meeting at His Glory when they were kids. They lived next door to each other and stuck together day in and day out. Their friends called them Stupid and Really Stupid though they both were the smartest in their class.

The first time they explored the skeleton yard, a dirty, silver key was sticking out of the lock of the Lyon's mausoleum. It was December 24th, and the graves were covered with a smelly mist that came from one of the cotton mills. Ben and Grace stole the key, but not before they crept inside to see what all the to-do was about. The Lyons, being the richest folks in town, had as big a house for their dead as they did for the living. It was bare and rather nippy inside. It had the sweet-sour smell of death, not just of red clay, but also of flowers, greenery, and smoke.

Grace and Ben moved their hands along the blue marble walls. Words were etched into the stone all around them like fortunes — The cream will rise to the top and into heaven. Our red-cheeked Sarah is now at rest. 1870-1888 - Sarah Catherine Lyon - Died January 5, 1888. *Or,* Sad in Life, Finally Happy at Rest - Richard King Lyon - Born October 13, 1901- Died October 29, 1926. *Beside him,* Tobacco is Our Blood. 1860-1912 - Samuel Luke Lyon. *Above him, but below Sarah,* God Works In His Own Way. Roscoe Samuel Lyon - Born January 5, 1888 - Died January 5, 1888.

Seeds

At sunrise Cane walks to work, unnoticed and undeterred by human contact. She takes various routes through town, hoping to catch a glimpse of some family moment. Last week, she saw all 16 of the Rayford kids clamoring around their living room, getting ready for school. She heard Jellie Rayford yell, "Biscuits, now!" Cane benefited from the way sound carried in the early morning in Marrow. She would be able to tell most of the goings on in the households she passed, even if she were blind. She loved other peoples' families. It was easy to conjure up images from the smells and sounds that jolted her senses. Though her profession required a keen eye, she had found that over the years, her nose and ears had improved her photography. She had wondered what her pictures would have been like if it were possible to capture the searing odor of humid red clay or the muted chatter between sweethearts.

She stops at the edge of a rain ditch near the Haydon home. Cane knows November is supposed to be chilly, your breath speaking ahead of your words, but not today. The early morning light is hazy and strange. Lily Haydon is in the front yard. Lily looks like a burst of sunshine. She is skinny with a head of white-blonde hair. Hiding behind a pair of double-flowering camellia bushes, Cane strains her neck to spy on her. Lily is digging holes in orderly rows. She wonders if Lily knows the meaning of the Sarah Frost's, the delicate pink blossoms separating her yard and the Ladders. *Longing for you.*

"Blueberry-seeds, bird-seeds, baby-seeds, angel-seeds." Lily

STEPHANIE M^CCOY / 44

drops something in each opening. She continues a quiet conversation with no one that Cane can see. "The birds will bring
back a new baby and I'll feed him with the blueberries and if he
dies Mama won't be sad again because the angels will take him
to heaven this time." Her chunky fingers pat down the earth
after each hole is filled. She pokes stick markers at the heads of
each row, with paper signs flapping as the thick morning breeze
pushes the scraggly labels back and forth. "King says the blue
baby is in a box near the rotten merry-go-round and that it
went straight to hell. Just because he's memorized all the plot
and street names in town doesn't mean he's smarter than me."

Cane recalls that the blue baby is near the old merry-go-
round. Cane had taken a glass eye from one of the carousel
horses that had pushed through the earth after a storm, the day
the blue baby was buried. King should know better. That baby
went to heaven like they all do. A lullaby wanders to the front
of her thoughts. The one that the woman from Durham told
her was Baby Ireni's favorite.

> *What'll we do with the baby?*
> *What'll we do with the baby?*
> *What'll we do with the baby?*
> *Oh, we'll wrap it up in calico,*
> *Wrap it up in calico,*
> *And send it to its pappy-o.*

Cane had whispered it to the baby before the mother had
put her back in her tiny coffin for the ride home. At the time,
she hadn't noticed the baby's calico outfit since the mother had
arrived in her wedding dress. It never occurred to Cane to ask
about the father.

"I hope they bury me near the circus," Lily says to her
imaginary pal. She gets up to go back into the house. Cane
makes circles around the skin where her neck aches from

crouching. Lily spins her head from side to side so her hair wraps around her face, catching a few strands in her mouth. Before she slips back into the Haydon home, she turns around and waves at Cane.

Cane backs away to the side of the house next door. Panic sets in when she is observed. Usually she is so careful, she is able to disappear before anyone notices her presence. One thing she has discovered about babies and children is that they have a different sense of who is nearby. They always register loss, but are just as good at sensing the presence of someone or something unexpected. Lily Haydon wasn't any different than most kids in Marrow. Her mother had tried to hide something that almost everyone knew about anyway. Even this youngest girl, who didn't really know what she spoke about, knew enough from the blood-clues she had inherited and bits of talk she had overheard. What child would really want to know, though, that her mother had a baby with someone else's husband here in town? What child would want to know that he was adopted because his mother couldn't have kids, because she drank herself barren with too many old vials of laudanum? What child would want to know her twin died next to her in her mother's womb? That was the latest tale that Eunice and her friends were passing around. Though Cane had to admit, when everything was said and done, she might want to know the truth; she'd want to know her past, so she could set her future.

Cane heads to Paw Creek, a small tributary of crystal water that feeds the Tear, to take a roundabout path to work, so she won't have to be seen again. On her way, she smells suffocating bacon fumes coming from one of the households she passes. They surround her and sink into her pores. She hates any variety of sizzling pig and the sludgy mess it leaves behind. It reminds her of Riley Trunk. Also, when she was younger, her mother smeared hog grease on her face to heal her facial defects. It didn't take.

Near the creek she wedges open weeping willow and creeper vines that will shield her from intruders. Here with the day already so moist and warm she decides to bathe, to remove the smell of pork unnoticed. At the edge of the water she washes her hands twice. The snakes and eater-bugs are nowhere in sight. They seem to migrate and stay content at the Tear. Maybe spirits of the Paw Creek Indians keep this part of their legacy free of harm.

Her saddle shoes clunk on the dirt. The tan bobby socks match the tan hide of her shoes in stark contrast to her chalky legs. The brown pleated skirt with pearl buttons is so stiff that when she steps out of it it stays standing. The buttons on her blouse are hidden and she digs inside the cotton flap to undo them. Her mother gave her five of these blouses,"to discourage any man who gets too fresh," she'd told Cane. But Cane overheard Mercy Haydon and Ulla Trunk say that these kinds of blouses were just the ones the Skeeter Grove boys loved to tussle with.

The morning sun spreads around the grove of trees at the creek. Cane unhooks her beige padded bra that is a hand-me-down from her mother. Cane doesn't need the extra stuffing, so it pinches to wear it all the time. Usually at her shop, with her work coat covering her day clothes, she removes her bra. Her white billowy underwear falls to her ankles. She flicks it high into the air with her foot like an acrobat at the circus and laughs. She is glad to be alone. The aching chill of the water is one of the few things that change the color of Cane's skin. The water at least feels and tastes like November, cool with a metallic sting on her tongue. She greets the thickest section of the creek as she quickly dips her body over and under its fast moving currents.

Standing in the web of sunrays that penetrate the vines, Cane shakes herself dry. From a distance she imagines she looks like a sea witch with her tangled hair, her jagged face, and her pulsing blue body. Cane looks down at herself. Her toes to her shoulders look OK. The blood in her veins has colored her skin enough, so she feels womanly. She is old enough. Old enough to be loved by someone. Her hand passes over her face. In the dark no one would see, she thinks, they would just love me. She hears the bobwhites calling and the factory whistle blow. She dresses efficiently, but leaves the top button of her blouse undone.

Inside her shop, Cane surveys the work for the day. Crop and touch up the Durham order, prepare two bodies from her mother's side, meet with the supply man from Kodak.

When Mr. Tatter died, Cane was the one to clean out his shop, the shop she came to own. She kept the name, Best Photography in Town because she believed one day that would be true for her, too. Mr. Tatter had the usual Civil War photographs, plantation daguerreotypes, fading tin types, and old busted cameras, a few of which were detective cameras. Cane regretted not knowing for what purposes Mr. Tatter had used those. Nothing was really hidden in Marrow, though the time King Lyon flubbed his lines playing Hamlet and said, "Something's rotten in Marrow," nobody laughed and some people in the audience just shook their heads, muttering, "Now there's a truth."

While she was sorting through his belongings, she came across jars of whole animals suspended in formaldehyde. It seemed Mr. Tatter fancied himself a biologist and often went to the farms in the greater Marrow area to collect oddities in nature. He labeled and dated each jar: *Siamese twin squirrels, Bernadette Farm, 1933.* Or, *Baby pig with three-foot tail, Pierce Plantation, 1890.* The tail was so long it had strangled the head of the piglet in the womb. Another was *Black-eyed mice family,*

Dewey Farm, 1929, a family of mice that had thick bulges circling each eye, like bull dogs or folks who had been beaten.

In the desk drawer mixed in with business papers, she found a cabinet card of dead triplets. They were in a lace-draped casket that was as wide as it was long. On the back someone had written *Mamma's little traitors*. There was another larger photograph in a file marked *Family*. It was a picture of a two-story home on a small hill. In front of the house was a large grass field scattered with coffins, some with classical lids, some with dome lids, and some without any covering, though grass was growing in the middle of a few. On the back of the mounting board, Mr. Tatter, Cane suspected, had written, *My Home—where I played and learned the dead trade—before I fell for the camera.* There was also a faded print she glanced at and then hid from sight.

Cane hears girls approaching her shop. She runs to the window and peers out. She keeps watch over the girls, to get ideas on how to be one. Mercy Haydon is talking at water-moccasin speed.

"Did you know the two Tommys were caught red-handed stealing wine from Miss Dunnet?" Mercy says to her friend Ulla Trunk. "According to the Bible, they are sinners, and according to the Reverend, they will go straight to Hell. Either you're a slave to God, the Reverend says, or you're a slave to sin."

Ulla is holding her body as if to barricade it. She turns toward Cane's shop and their eyes catch before Cane lets the curtain cover her.

If a man Cane hated died today, she would still sing his body a lullaby. Cane may hate the live person, but the dead body was to be comforted, especially the children. If a child dies in wintertime, Cane wraps a blanket around it.

For the children without parents or the children whose

parents couldn't name a favorite song, or hadn't had enough cradle-time to sing one, Cane would offer,

> *Baby dear, Baby dear,*
> *Don't you cry,*
> *Father will come to you bye and bye,*
> *Mother is baking you cakes to eat.*

before putting the preserved child back in a coffin. But that won't do for Riley Trunk.

Old Verse
(1930s)

*R*iley had tried hard to snare Darleen Walker with his greasy smile shortly after he and his child-bride Rachel had married. It didn't matter that Darleen was night courting Buckford Kent. Even if Riley weren't married, if his family had known he was favoring Marrow's mortician, he would have been shipped off to the crazy farm, so he sought her out at night just like Buckford.

One evening at His Glory, Riley had heard her and Buckford reciting something at a grave. When he got closer he saw the remains had bubbled up above ground. A split thighbone and three ribs dangled over the coffin.

"I lived, I loved, I quaff'd, like thee:
I died: let earth my bones resign:
Fill up — thou canst not injure me;
The worm has fouler lips than thine."

Darleen paused. She had heard a noise and turned to see Riley approaching.

"What brings you here, Mr. Trunk?"

"Didn't mean any disrespect, Miss Walker. I didn't know there had been another passing in town." Riley ignored Buckford Kent and let all his wits focus on Miss Walker. He had adored her for a good while, but his duty to Rachel kept him from straying too far. Yet this meeting and a few other chance meetings gave him a sense of pride in what could be. "I didn't recognize the scripture, but it sounded so pure."

"Yes, pure it is," replied Darleen covering her mouth. Buckford had looked away and was having a coughing fit. Riley teetered his eyes at him. What does she see in him? Death looks healthier than that sack of skin. As Buckford continued to cough, Darleen stepped over to him and placed her hand on his back. And though Riley would have loved to feel her hand running down his spine, he noticed that Buckford's cough intensified as she rubbed his skin.

"Mr. Trunk, we are saying good-bye to an old friend. Would you care to toast to his good health with us?" Darleen handed a skull cup to Riley. Riley was terrified to taste the liquid inside, but with Buckford Kent nearby he didn't want to show himself yellow.

"While you drink, I'll serenade you with more scripture." As Riley took a tiny sip, or rather, he touched the liquid and let it fall back into the bone bowl, Darleen spoke.

"Quaff while thou canst: another race,
When thou and thine, like me are sped,
May rescue thee from earth's embrace,
And rhyme and revel with the dead."

Not being a Bible-reading man, Riley waited a pious moment and then handed the wine back to Darleen. He touched her hand on purpose. "Miss Walker, your hand needs warming." Why didn't Buckford heat up her hands? Riley would, if Darleen would give him half the chance. Buckford was too busy fussing with his broken-down body.

"They say cold hands mean a warm heart," Darleen replied. "Just my luck this evening to have two gentleman suitors."

Buckford exhaled and crossed one of his arms over his chest. Riley held his breath. "Now I want you both to close your eyes. I'm handing out kisses tonight.

With his eyes closed, Riley heard Buckford giggle. "Now, Darleen," Buckford said, and then he seemed to go silent.

"What'd you do to him, Miss Walker? I hope your kisses aren't lethal."

Riley felt Darleen guide him forward. "Deadly, Mr. Trunk. Buckford wasn't feeling too well, so he went home. Now step up," she said. "Step up. We need some room for romance." Riley stepped over a board and felt his foot roll over a bone and squish into soft dirt.

"Now if you turn around a bit and hold my hand, I'll scratch your back for you, before we commence." Riley obliged and Darleen took her time scratching his back with a rough stick. "Got to get around your ribs here. Now keep those eyes shut, Mr. Trunk. I don't like cheaters."

Whatever Riley was stepping on had oozed around his feet. Though his shoes protected him, he felt a penetrating dampness coupled with a rank smell. He pointed his nose upwards trying to decipher the odor.

"Don't worry Mr. Trunk. It's decayed bone marrow. It stays with the body forever. You can smell it all over town." Darleen let go of his hand. She undid his pants with precision and they fell to his knees. She touched his body with the scratching stick.

"Ah, Miss Walker," Riley said wondering where this encounter would lead. Something kissed his chin and then his chest. It was soft like a newborn chick. Riley was full ready to lay down with Darleen, if she desired, but even a few more kisses would do.

"Bones make the best scratchers and worms the best kissers."

Darleen shoved Riley backwards and he fell half over the coffin. His pants tangled up his legs as his back and head hit the ground. He heard her run off.

"Buckford, Buckford, I got that cheater good!" Darleen said loud enough for most people dead or alive in town to hear.

When Riley tried to reach his arms to his legs to release himself, his shirt buttons snagged on his pants. He was stranded there, hog-tied.

Picture Perfect

Cane looked over the shots hanging on the line of Baby Ireni and her mother. She cropped the white edges, stood back and lined up the best ones in a row. The white dress had distracted her more than she'd thought. Baby Ireni's mouth was open in most of the photographs. Her mother was crying, but her eyes were closed and that worked out fine. Baby Ireni held a doll in a matching dress. Cane had missed that. As her mother clutched her, the dead child held the doll she'd never dress or have tea with, in a rigor-mortis grip. At least the flowers looked good in her other hand. Cane could have tampered with the picture, she could have added color here and there to change the image from what it was, but she never did that. Her mother gussied-up the bodies, but Cane never asked her subjects to be any more than what they were when they walked or were pushed into her shop. She would clear up a mistake on her part, a tiny scratch on the negative or a mark on the paper. There was the rare occasion when she used a pencil to fill in the negative, to lighten the print, or a scalpel to scrape away at the negative with her feather touch to darken it. Most professional photographers had an easel that they tilted to correct for distortion, but that didn't count and Cane rarely used it.

At her viewing table she chose the four best shots, stamped the business mark on the back of each one, wrapped them in special mailing paper, and slid them into a slender box she had already labeled for the postman to take to Durham. The Kodak man would be arriving any moment. The two bodies her mother wanted photographed would have to wait until later. They were Presbyterian Old Folks Home bodies. They had died within hours of each other. Probably people her mother had been eyeing for months. Cane was sad for the babies that died, but the passing of the old people in Marrow was not mournful to her. She just hoped they had been fed their favorite food, or heard an earmarked passage from the Bible. Near the end, it seemed to her that most people just wanted the simple things they had enjoyed in life — a crispy chicken wing, a box of Martha Washington candies, and visitors that came often but didn't stay too long.

At noon, many of the church organists played the cherished hymns of the recently deceased. Because it was close to Thanksgiving the music was extra loud.

Right as the Kodak man walked in her door, Cane heard the sounds of "Rock of Ages" at the Baptists in a contest with "Jesus Loves Me" from the Presbyterians and "For the Beauty of the Earth" from the Methodists.

"Gosh, it's hard to keep your head straight with that racket," said Mr. Kincaid. He took off his hat. "Sorry, Miss Walker, I didn't mean any disrespect." His ears had a bounty of hairs growing out of them.

He had been selling camera supplies to Cane for years. She referred to him as the Kodak man, but he sold supplies from all the companies. Slowly she had let him see her face. He either was half-blind — he did wear thick glasses — or, in his traveling-salesman world, he'd seen so much that the sight of Cane didn't make him pause.

"I like it better when just one of the churches plays," Cane said.

"Well, me, too." He put down his sagging leather bag and rummaged through it. Cane always noticed the widening bald spot on his head. It looked tender and foreign. The urge to touch it never subsided. If she had some bat blood she'd smear it on his head to rekindle his head roots. She didn't have much opportunity to observe the heads of live men.

"I know you aren't interested in the color tinting supplies I have, but there's a new paper out that makes your pictures come alive. It's a high glossy paper that almost speaks by itself. My other accounts from Richmond to Atlanta love the results. It's especially good for weddings," said Mr. Kincaid. He remained at the front of the store near Cane's desk, aware that he wasn't invited to go any further into the shop. "You must get a lot of wedding business."

"I did have some a while back, but my mother and the families in the area keep me busy. Haven't time for that kind of business now."

"A lot of my accounts ordered some for their own weddings." Mr. Kincaid said and stopped right as he sounded out the "ings" of his sentence. His facial expression was trapped in a clown smile. A purplish-red color moved across Cane's cheeks and met at her forehead. Mr. Kincaid bent over like a worm and dug into his bag, almost catching his glasses. They bounced out of his wobbly grasp and thudded on the wooden boards. The lenses were so thick, they saved themselves from shattering.

"Look here, Miss Walker," he said as he straightened up, "I brought you some free samples. Let me know if you want any more of these."

"Thank you, Mr. Kincaid, I'll just have my usual order this time and you can bring the same when you return. I don't expect any changes."

Mr. Kincaid wasn't known to linger in her shop. Cane's phone rang, and he waited patiently for her to finish. He bid Cane farewell and departed before the war of the hymns ended.

Cane looked over the free samples — perfume to add to the water bath to enhance a special occasion shot, a small scrapbook in the shape of a camera, and despite her protests he'd left a sample of the wedding paper, and a circular stamp and pad that had her name written on it — *Photographs by Cane Walker.* It never occurred to her to put her name on her photographs. She still used Mr. Tatter's stamp that read: *The Best Photographs in Town, Marrow, NC.* Cane stamped her left hand and then the other. All the way up her arm she made a train of stamps. They looked like the tattoos she'd seen on some servicemen. After her arm dried she bent her face over and kissed it. The skin on her arm was smooth and tiny brown hairs tickled her lips.

"Whom are you practicing for?" Darleen Walker said as she rolled two bodies she'd squished onto one gurney into Cane's shop. There were many times Cane wished she'd closed off the doorway between their businesses. Too often her mother charged in when Cane was having a few moments of peace.

"Let's go on and get a shot of the best friends and then I can get them to their homes for the visitation tonight, or maybe you have plans with your new beau."

Cane almost responded and then just shook her head. How could there be anyone? A beau? She and her mother moved the bodies onto the daybed. Cane didn't usually photograph the deceased elderly. Most folks didn't want those kinds of keepsakes. But these two women had been best chums, dying within hours of each other; they had stipulated in their wills that a photograph be taken and put in each other's coffins. Cane was able to prop them up with pillows and have them hold hands. Her mother had overdone the make-up, but Cane was probably the only one who would notice that.

"Aren't they a pair?" Darleen said. "College sweethearts."

"They went to college?" Cane asked. She had wanted to go to college some day. Cane took a moment to check the light. She took Kate Greenway's *The Language of Flowers* and put it on the side of one of the women. She set *Sonnets from the Portuguese* by Elizabeth Barrett Browning in the empty hand of the other best friend.

"Peace College," Darleen said. "That place where all the rich folk send their girls with bubbling brains and breasts. Lot of good it did these two."

Cane knew of other morticians around the state. They weren't a bit like her mother. They respected the dead and the science of their profession. She knew of no other mother like hers.

Cane took a few shots of the ladies. By herself she lifted one body onto the gurney, while her mother helped herself to the supplies from the Kodak salesman. Cane pushed the corpse into her mother's shop, returned it to its coffin and went back to fetch the other body. If she ever did have a boyfriend, she'd keep that news to herself. She'd be ready, though, when it did happen. She'd sent away for a book that would help her uncover what she didn't know about men and women together.

Alone together.

A Day of Feasts
(1941)

Grace made her husband Rolland a beet sandwich for the drive to Aberdeen. He always went to visit his kin the morning of Christmas Eve, returning for midnight service at the Presbyterian Church. Grace never went with him or had to worry about any of his ironing. Rolland took his shirts home to Aberdeen where his mother's maid ironed and starched them stiff as dead bodies. Early on it was clear she was too independent for the Haydon family, especially the womenfolk. Grace had trouble visiting Rolland's family and sitting still and being unobtrusive, like the other Haydon women. Grace talked about European geography, politics outside of North Carolina, and croquet, a game she still played weekly with her father. She talked so much; people would get up and leave the room.

For her part, Grace was delighted to have the time to herself to spend how she liked. As she had for years, she bundled up and headed to the marble house for her annual toast to the past.

It wasn't her year to decorate the solid structure, so she concentrated on Yuletide delicacies: Christmas Eve Good Luck Dip, Hunter Clark's Barded Birds, Great Aunt Nettie's Sweet Potato Casserole, Pookie's Milk Punch and a plate of buttered biscuits. Even though she had married Rolland, she couldn't bring herself to break the ritual of meeting Ben Ladder. It was the only secret left that they shared. She felt that it was their Christmas gift to each other, a childhood remembrance. A part of her knew it was wrong, but her tie to Ben was stronger than her marriage. Each year they arrived like starved calves and went home like stuffed hogs.

"In honor of the owner of the house, I made candleholders out of

61

tobacco leaves," Ben said, as Grace stepped past the intricate iron gate and through the wooden door with a dogwood flower carved in the center. The color of the flower, once painted white, had peeled away to the black oak underneath.

Ben Ladder had arrived at the marble house an hour before Grace. He wanted to make the inside a holiday wonderland. And with all the candles set into the areas for vases and urns, the room radiated piercing firelight.

Grace tried not to be consumed by the joy in his eyes, the way the light bounced off the names of the dead, the way the marble house became warmer and warmer like a tropical infection.

On Christmas Eve, Ina Ladder spent a good portion of the day helping the Presbyterian minister get the church ready for the evening celebrations. Her newlywed-husband Ben had a Christmas project to finish. Ina made sure, too, that the afternoon Last-Minute Holiday Bazaar was stocked with enough items for those church members who waited until the very end, or those who had received their paychecks only that morning.

She gazed around the church basement. Tables were set up and women were arranging angel ornaments made out of cotton clusters, dried tobacco wreaths, silk handkerchiefs, red Bibles, Confederate dolls that had a lady of the house on one end and colored servant girl on the flip side. She admired these women of the church, who gave and gave of their time every Sunday and especially during the religious holidays. She was blessed to work in the Lord's house with the other ladies by her side. There were jams and jellies that had knitted socks to hold them; there was an abundance of holiday sweets. Ina had made three Christmas Scripture cakes that everyone agreed were better than the ones at the Methodists or Baptists. Her cakes, however, quietly competed with the Cuffee sisters' Communist Tea cookies. No one could resist them, much as they tried. One bite into the fat middle and a *fermented cherry would burst open, and the sinful liqueur the Cuffee sisters put up every year, oozed out.*

In addition, this year Ina had donated a birth quilt that showed a patchwork of the life of Jesus with the hand-stitched words at the top: Jesus Loves the Little Children. She had to admit one of the reasons why she spent the day at the church was that she wanted to see who bought the quilt, to get a clue as to who might be blessed in the spring or summer. Her only regret was that her husband Benjamin couldn't come with her. The ladies kept asking about him, just like people in town had kept hinting to her about children.

Ben and Grace hadn't tasted any of the food. There was only one candle still lit and it was starting to burn the leaves of the holder. The candy smell of tobacco filled the room and the smoke clouded above the soft, birdlike gulps that Ben and Grace made. Their limbs were rivers, intertwined, fluid.

"Things will change," Grace said. She knew Ben had seen her naked body from her bathroom window that was neighbor-to-neighbor with his. She didn't turn around to put on her clothes.

Ben took a knife from one of the platters and stooped at the bottom corner of the blue marble wall. He motioned her to him and held Grace's hand over his as he carved out the letters of their names.

"Something was meant to."

Class Photo Day

Thursday was Class Photo Day and Cane had a full session of work ahead of her. She was substituting for Mr. Holt, who normally handled the school photos. He was convinced he was afflicted with Marrow Madness as folks were beginning to call it, but really he had just come down with a bad case of the flu. The kind of flu that makes your skin look green and you wish you were headed for His Glory. So he'd called Cane in a fevered panic, and with his gelatinous voice had pleaded with her to step in. One of her New Year's resolutions for 1958 was to try to be kinder to people she didn't like, so she said yes.

Cane had hired her mother's assistant Wilbert to help her so that she could stay behind the camera and concentrate, though every one of the high school kids knew it was also because she didn't want anyone to see her. But Cane was adamant that she would do her best. The saying, Saturday's child works hard for a living, was true for Cane. The only other person Cane knew who had been born on a Saturday was Jack Pliney, and he worked harder than all the residents of Marrow combined.

When she had the opportunity, Cane enjoyed photographing live babies and toddlers because they hadn't decided how someone should look. But by the time kids got to high school many of them had decided — or they just wanted to be mean about life. A lot of the girls thought they were the only stitch in a dress. Some of the teenage boys in town had already tried menacing ways to get Cane to show herself. Dead people were a lot less trouble.

The kids started arriving at 10 a.m. They were allowed to leave school and walk down Main Street to her shop. There was a teacher at the school gate to make sure they headed in the right direction, and one at the entrance to Cane's shop to make sure they actually went in for the photo session.

The group today was the juniors. There were 12 scheduled, plus 2 guests. The class originally had 15, but one boy had killed himself walking on the train tracks between Marrow and Skeeter Grove. It had been reported as an accident, but there were three witnesses that said he had run straight toward the train with his arms set for a fight. The two other juniors that would not be having their pictures taken were Cynthia Duke and Willa Sanders. One was a pearly girl and the other was the daughter of the president of Loyal Tobacco Company. The only thing the two had in common was that they both had visited Granny Ma'am just after summer ended. Granny Ma'am fixed things that others wouldn't. It seemed the two girls were each so scared of what might happen to them if their bellies grew that they drank twice the amount of cotton root and tansy tea Granny Ma'am had given them. Instead of the potion cleansing out one life, it cleansed out all life.

A few weeks later Granny Ma'am passed. There were rumors that the tobacco families had her done up, but she died a natural death. The only trouble was that no one knew whom she belonged to. She was a lot of people mixed into one. No one knew for sure what color she was. She'd mixed in with every race since she opened for business. Even the Cuffee sisters remembered her as being well established in Marrow when they first arrived with the circus.

When she was dying, Granny Ma'am lay down on the patch of earth near her cabin and tried to scratch herself a grave. The noise was so loud, a neighbor down the way heard the clawing in the clay. Darleen was called to come get her, but by the time she arrived Granny Ma'am had disappeared. Darleen reported back to Cane, and anyone who questioned her about it, that she had heard the scratch-scratch noise all around her coming from the water oak and the pokeweed, but there wasn't a body to be found. If there had been, Darleen would have hissed it out.

They arrived two-by-two. Cane had been given a list of names, but she'd known of these kids for years. Nella and Minish were first. Nella was a year younger than Minish, but she had been put a year ahead when she started reading in kindergarten. Cane knew the two of them the best from her visits to see Jack Pliney. They never spoke to her, but they responded if she used their finger code. They were the only colored kids in the whole school. Mr. Lyon insisted they be let in; not because it was the law but because Hurricane Hazel had made him rethink a few things about the world. Then it was Mitty Hyde's girl, Sally, and Josiah Mitchell. Emmaline's girl, Betsey, and her best friend, Ruth, whose mother ran the florist shop followed. Mercy Haydon and Ulla Trunk rounded out the mid-section. Melinda Green, who lived on the outskirts of Marrow and was the only person in her house who made it to high school, and Walter Graham, whose Daddy worked at the bank, were a pair. Tommy Rayford and Tommy West were next. The guests, Eunice Lyon and her cousin King were last in the line though Eunice refused to walk side-by-side with King. He dawdled behind knowing better than to try to equal himself with Eunice, even though he was older. Mr. Lyon had arranged for Cane to take his picture at the same time as Eunice. The teacher, Mr. Benson, waited outside, smoking a cigarette. Cane had heard him say to the group before they entered her shop, "Now, y'all be nice to Miss Cane, and try not to stare at her face."

Cane had prepared the backdrop for the day. The lighting was set. She would adjust for each face. The plates were ready to be loaded by her side. She had hung a print of the angel of peace with a child clutching her neck for all the kids to gaze at.

They would be looking just off center. She found that direction produced the best results. The print had come from the Kodak supply man. He knew the bulk of her business was death portraits, so he'd given it to her. She laughed now to think that she was using it to keep live people from looking her way.

Wilbert motioned Nella over to sit down. Cane could tell she had tried hard to look older than her years. Cane knocked her hand on the camera front. Her face and body were hidden behind a black drape and the bulk of her camera. Hair out of your mouth, she finger-coded to Nella. Nella sighed and then slowly pulled the hair out. "Now, look to the angel," Cane said. Cane took one shot and motioned Wilbert for the next one. Each girl was wearing a sweater, and they all seemed to have spent their Christmas money at Emmaline's Beauty Parlor. Emmaline had become one of the most successful beauticians in the county because when she was just getting started, she'd given away haircuts to the sorriest-looking girls. The results were so miraculous that girls with only half-sorry looks would line up and pay.

On this day most of the girls had long locks down the sides with a hair wave over the top, except for those who had just had a permanent. The curls on their heads were so tight it hurt to look at them. Nella had tried to straighten her hair by using Madame C. J. Walker's products. Only Minish had kept hers short like a movie star. The two Tommys had decided to wear matching shirts and they parted their hair far over to the side, so that a large amount fell over one eye. The detective look, Cane thought.

"As a favor to your mother," Cane said, "could you move your hair away from your eyes?" Tommy Ray scowled but complied, though he took his time. Tommy West was asked the same thing. "No, ma'am." he replied. "I worked all morning to get this just right, and this is how I want to be remembered. ... Ma'am." Cane saw Wilbert roll his eyes. "Is there any trouble, Miss Cane?" Mr. Kent called out through a shield of smoke. "Eyes towards the angel, Tommy." Cane loaded the new plate and snapped away. "Don't blame me if your folks are upset with you." Tommy stuck his fingers in the mass of hair falling over his face. He twisted the hair back. He stood up and came towards the camera. "They won't be upset with me; they'll be upset with you." He put his eye up to the eye of the camera. "I've never been with an ugly girl, but they say they are the best," he whispered before Wilbert could get to him and move him along.

When Eunice had her turn, she took five minutes getting herself ready. "Don't see why Mr. Holt couldn't have rescheduled," she said to her friends. She put the tips of her painted nails to her cheeks and rubbed her hands back and forth like she was washing her face. "My Ponds cream works wonders." Cane clicked her through without a word. Cane would have ample opportunity to recreate Eunice's face if she desired. Wilbert escorted Eunice to the door.

"I didn't die, so Mama would never let me come here." King said. He walked up to the camera and tapped on it like it was a front door. "Miss Cane, if you take my picture, will I die? The other babies did. And Joe Monroe cut off his toe."

"King. You'll be all right." Cane told him. "Everybody needs a picture of themselves, even if they're alive."

Merciful Hysteria
(1951)

O n Cane Walker's sixteenth birthday, her mother gave her a subscription to Popular Photography and a pound cake that was better than fresh, as Darleen said. The first issue arrived in June. Darleen had it sent to Cane's shop so she could start learning more about other areas of the business, especially salesmanship. Cane suspected her mother wanted her to branch out — still shots, nature studies, in-home portraiture, the latter of which Cane could never see herself pursuing — to bring in more money.

The postman dropped her mail through the slot of the front door. The slapping of the wooden lip and the way the mail hit the floor startled Cane every day. It was an intrusion, though she coveted the twice daily bits of news, orders, advertisements, and an occasional penny postcard from folks who didn't know Mr. Tatter had passed away.

The new magazine fell open when it cascaded to the floor. "She Photographed Her Own Operation." The title was in bold letters. Cane picked up the thick periodical and began reading. Who would ever photograph themselves? The woman, Mary Eleanor Browning, had taken 108 pictures of herself while being operated on. After she had been injected with morphine.

"Mother! Mother!" Cane yelled through the walls between their shops. She scratched at the wall with her nails. The woman had a dangerous tumor. She read through the article. The woman photographer had attached a large mirror to a lamp so she could record in pictures her day in the hospital. Cane was riveted and impressed. Boy, wouldn't Grace Haydon hate that. She had no mirrors in her home. Mercy Haydon lingered at Rose's Department store just to get a good *solid look at herself. The woman's body, facial features, and emotions were on display not only for her to photograph, but also in full view of the doctors and nurses. Cane herself didn't have a mirror in her room at home and only had a beaded one for her customers in her shop. Who would allow such madness? And where was the tumor located?*

From the photographs, Cane thought at first it might be in her stomach. But the way the woman sat up and the way her legs were opened while she shot a self-portrait made Cane squirm. Scissors holding the incision closed stuck out at odd angles, while a white cloth unsuccessfully covered the woman's private area. She could see the surgeon's hands set to continue the procedure, to continue cutting the woman's body.

Darleen came into the shop with her hands reeking of formaldehyde and borax. Just at that moment Cane realized the woman was making a picture book of her own hysterectomy.

"Cane! What is it? I'm right in the middle of Everette Oliver."

Cane started to tell her mother, but her excitement of the initial idea had plummeted into embarrassment and disgust.

"Thank you for the magazine subscription." Cane closed the issue and showed her the cover, careful not to expose any pages.

It was bad enough to have an operation. Worse, Cane imagined, to lose your female parts. Who are you without your female parts?

"The way you called out to me, Cane. I thought you were in hysterics over something. Merciful Hysteria is what my mother called it, because the thrust of it could clear out your feeling chamber and then you'd be quiet for a long spell. Yours must be flat empty by now." Darleen pouted in a way that made her face look lopsided.

"But to my ear it's just a pack of catty women hollering out of one body."

"Mother, what is a hysterectomy?" Cane thought she knew, but her mother would know the whole of it.

Darleen laughed. "Who put that word in your brain?" She shook her gloved hands and bits of chemical drops landed on Cane's stomach marking her clothes.

Stepping back to avoid further contamination, Cane turned her face toward the tear in the curtains in the front of her shop.

"It's no secret or anything. They slice you open and take out your womb and the connected parts. Usually older women have it done, when they are all used up."

Though her mother didn't live a truthful life, when Cane asked her a question, she answered with the truth.

"Now, I was figuring I needed to start worrying about you and boys. Here you come talking about the end of it all. What a wonder. Was it those Cuffee sisters that put that notion in your head?"

Cane shook her head. If she told her mother where she learned about it, Cane worried that Darleen might cancel her subscription. Darleen liked to be the keeper of the truth; she didn't respond well when Cane learned about the world from other people or things.

Cane was repelled by and drawn to the article, but the newness of the magazine, the possibilities outside Marrow attracted her the most.

"Grandma Winnie spoke about it one time." Cane looked down at her blouse and saw that the chemicals had eaten away at it like moths feasting on wool, as if the lying was catching up with her.

"I guess one of her lady friends had trouble . . ." Cane looked at her mother and then focused on a small opening between the floorboards.

"Down there."

"No disrespect to my own mother, but she and her lady friends had babies as often as rabbits breed. As if they were trying to win a blue ribbon at the Harvest Fair. Pop, pop, pop. And then there were a dozen young-uns needing your time."

Cane let the conversation end. She could have asked her mother if that was why she only had one child. But Cane wasn't sure she wanted to hear her answer.

Her mother returned to Everette Oliver.

The chemicals had slowly burned onto Cane's skin. So slowly that she didn't notice the new marks on her body until she undressed that evening for bed. If she could have moved the markings on her face to *other parts of her body she would, even if it meant that the rest of her body was damaged. No matter who you are, Cane thought to herself, your face is the first thing people see, if they can see at all. Even blind people feel your face when they first meet you. When you're born everybody wants to see what you look like. Cane would gladly get a hysterectomy, if it would clear up her face.*

King of the Hill

King, the wispy, bow-legged son of Henry Lyon, was often seen spying on Nella and Minish, the two colored girls who lived on his parents' property. The dogwood-tree-lined land sat propped upon a hill overlooking Marrow and the snaky Tear River. King would collect the blossoms and make a bed in the garden. The dogwood was especially noteworthy, since it was useful to canine and man alike when brewed to cure mange or other parasitic ailments, but most folks just liked the look of it. King would roll back and forth until he was surrounded by its scent.

The mansion had two rows of dwarf cedars leading up to the main doorway. The front porch had a trellis of American Pillar roses mixed in with the hard to maintain but odoriferous Confederate jasmine. *Hibiscus mutabilis* previously overran the property, but King's mother was much offended by the way that their virgin-white color changed to fleshy pink and then to deathly red as they aged. History had it that the property had been a tobacco plantation gone bust when the first Lyon in Marrow brought his bride-to-be from England, a portly, cream-fed Cotswold girl weighing in at 223 pounds. She had been bartered for tobacco pound for pound, and the plantation went under over the deal.

The Lyon family seemed to have recouped their losses, however, and was now the richest family in Marrow. Nella and Minish lived with their families near the back pond in houses that shimmered at night like celestial shrines. The gardener

Jack Pliney lived in what was once the chapel, though it had been abandoned at the end of the Civil War.

Though King was older than Nella and Minish, he loved playing children's games with them and fancying himself a spy for the United States of America. He was slow in the head except he knew all the names of the streets in town and the plots at the cemetery. He could rattle them off from A to Z.

Today, with a smudge of the Wolf Moon still visible, King and the two girls were practicing kick-the-can, using a tarnished Gorham silver champagne bucket that King's mother had thrown out the window one evening in the 1940s, instead of her son. On that night, King had been wandering the property when he noticed a white woman slip into Jack Pliney's home. Though in the pecking order of servants a gardener was near the bottom, to King's father he had become the most valuable worker. Jack Pliney was part colored and part clay-colored, but King could never figure out exactly what two colors Pliney's folks had used to make him the color he was. He looked like the red clay from the yard and the sorghum pudding the cook made whenever King's parents were away.

Jack Pliney had just lost his wife in childbirth. It was difficult enough to work for King's father — even King knew that — but to have an infant to care for without its mother was more weight than Jack Pliney could bear. Or that's what King's mother had told him. "My God, my God, why hast thou forsaken me?" Jack Pliney had said to the body of his dead wife, but everyone on the property could hear him wail, over and over, like an injured horse. Word was sent out that Baby Faith was in need of a wet nurse. The other servants found one by chance: a mother who had recently lost her own.

Though only five years old at the time, King had pronounced himself a detective and snuck around to the gardener's house, peering into the window of the one-room home with the wooden t hanging in the back. Inside, the hooded white woman had uncovered her breasts, which were full like the tetherball hanging by King's back porch. She fed the baby and King watched as the milk spilled out of her other breast like falling stars, watched as the baby sucked and sucked, coughing and choking on every drop, and pawing like a kitten with its nubby hand at the other breast. Pliney sat with his back to them and even King could not see the expression on his face.

"Mee-ma, Mee-ma!" King cried after he had removed himself from hearing range and fled with delight into his home, calling his mother a name that really meant grandmother but had stuck since he mumbled his first words. King always imagined a different woman than the one he was approaching, hopeful each time that she would transform herself into the mother he had always wished for.

"I want to taste that, your milky way," he said upon reaching her. King's mother lived in a wing of the mansion separate from the rest of the family. It was the only way, King's father had told King, that he could keep her safe from the Tear River ghosts. "I want to see white stars falling."

Before he'd finished the last syllable, he smelled the thickness of wine, the way it permeated the room and made him feel weak as if he pushed against storm winds.

His mother slapped him into the wood paneling, where his head made a mark that appeared to add texture to the grain. She would have thrown him out the window, but the first thing in reach was a sterling bucket, one of five she and Mr. Henry King Lyon had received as wedding gifts, and she grabbed that and yanked it around before pitching it and yelling to anyone in the neighborhood who cared to listen. The metal crashing onto the clay dirt made a thud and then a crackle as the ice splattered.

"Extracting. You men are always extracting," she had said and shoved him out of her section of the mansion, slamming the door so vehemently that it bounced back open and she had to slam it two more times for the latch to stick.

King stood staring at the worn door. Confusion set in, not because she had refused his request or slapped him, but because she had referred to him as a man.

The next evening after supper, when he had tried to talk to Jack Pliney about the white woman on their property, the confusion persisted.

"Son, you must never mention the visit from Miss Haydon. Folks don't talk about those kinds of things. They don't want to hear about it. Some go crazy when they do, you hear."

King nodded, not wanting to increase the population of crazy people in town, since there was already the Tear River ghost who captured snakes bare-handed out of the river. King had seen the ghost take off her shoes and walk barefooted through the watercress at the edge of the water and keep walking until she was up to her thighs. Her face was painted like an Indian warrior. The sharp current and cold water didn't bother her, nor did the tree roots that had to cut at her toes. She'd put one hand in the river and waited, and waited, sometimes a full hour before she'd pulled out a shining whip snake or a mean, fighting moccasin.

Then there was the entire Rayford family who refused to eat meat, just down the way, so King nodded again about keeping quiet, but still he couldn't fathom why anyone would refuse a plate of BBQ, or why Miss Haydon had milk to spare.

Jack Pliney moved away from King's questioning and began pruning a diseased tree, its fruit all swollen and misshapen, like a sprain. King's father had kept Pliney on because he was an expert when it came to curing diseased fruits, plants, and soil. On the Lyon property a lot needed fixing.

With Jack Pliney's back to him again that day, too, King couldn't see his face, though King thought he saw water drip off Pliney's clay-colored ears.

I'm going to be the best detective, King had said to himself. He had caught a few fireflies and then held them softly against the inside of his palm, watching the blinking beetles light up the dark cup of his hand.

Nowadays King wasn't as skilled catching fireflies. Nella and Minish were better at playing kick-the-can and he knew that on occasion they just let him win. He also knew there was something about him that wasn't quite complete, though Mitty Hyde had complimented him when he'd told her where the Graham family plot was located and the fastest route to get there from the highway. Nella and Minish were growing up and he just stayed where he was.

Still, he loved the affection his mother bestowed on his forehead on occasion, especially after he retrieved her daily coke cleanser from Winkie Sr.'s Soda Shop.

In town, some of the boys made fun of him. He didn't let their words harm him, but one comment in particular had stuck in his mind.

"King," one boy had said, "you just slosh around like pot-licker in a poor dog's belly."

Winkie Jr., Winkie Sr.'s son, was part of the crowd and had told the boy to shut up but laughed inside so that his Adam's apple bobbed. King could tell that much.

Mostly, though, when King thought about the phrase it made him sad for the dog.

Family Album 1956
(Miss Lily)

*M*y mother was heading for the border, that is, South Carolina. She'd just had a fight with Daddy over tadpoles. A tadpole was their code for having another baby. My mother rolled me up in her arm like a carnival ride and sat me in the front of our DeSoto and we careened out of Tar Heel country. That is until we hit the bear. I was six. Mercy was having a sleep-over at Eunice's, so she missed it all. She missed a lot around here, especially when she was listening to her Golden Meditations for Family Devotions that Reverend Mitchell had given her. She was like a shepherd that had no idea what her sheep were up to. Daddy would whisper to Mother that Mercy was Bible rich and feeling poor. He said I was just trouble with too much brain.

Mother got out of the car and walked higgledy-piggledy. The impact had rearranged all of us, including the car. I jumped out and ran over to the furry mass open like an empty swing.

"What's that thing between its foot-paws?" I asked. My mother, much embarrassed by public incidents but not bodies, said sideways, "That is his pee-paw. Your father has one too, although his is smaller."

"Poor thing," I said.

A truck approached our predicament and stopped right next to us. Triplet brothers were in the front seat crammed together. Once I wished for an older brother, but nothing came of it. I also wished my sister would disappear and she did on occasion, but only if she was invited somewhere else.

"Ma'am, is there anything we can do?"

"The bear is dead," said my mother and she motioned for me to skedaddle back into our dented car. I walked up to those boys who had scrambled out of their truck and had begun dragging the burly thing into the back opening of their Ford. They were fighting over each piece of it. I imagined they wanted to cook it up into BBQ.

"How big is your pee-paw?"

They all laughed.

"Our Daddy's six feet tall." They said this in unison like choirboys.

"Lily! Now!" my mother said and I walked backwards and sunk into the front seat. I shook my head wondering how older boys could be so dumb.

Diaphanous Desire

The one item Cane took from Mr. Tatter's leftovers that she never told anyone about was the Japanese print. And it wasn't really thievery since Darleen had been left the entire shop, but Cane felt like a thief. The faded print of a man and woman facing each other made her body coil. Since the man and the woman were looking so close, set to kiss, their expressions were hidden. In fact, though both their clothes were askew and his kimono robe was draped over her left leg, which was exposed up to her thigh, no one could say it was a naked picture. Cane could have lived off the nourishing stirrings it gave her, the desire of desire.

The man held a fan and his hand came over the hill of the woman's left shoulder with some of his fingers marching and others curling in the same instant. The woman was wearing three dress robes and a large shawl around her middle. Cane knew that everyone in Japan wore silk day in and day out. The woman's thumb and index finger were below the man's ear and on his chin respectively. If Cane thought about it too much, stared at it too long, she was sure neither of them was wearing undergarments. Though the lower edge of the print had faded worse than the rest, she was convinced that part of the woman's bottom might have originally been in view. But overall the private areas were not visible. Each face was out of view, not due to shame but to passion. There was something, too, about the way the material draped over the bodies, about the position of the open fan with black writing going up and down, and about the way the man grasped the woman's skin, that would at times force Cane to return the print to the lock-box in the secret drawer of her desk, where it resided at the moment.

Cane was a collector of desire. Even though Valentine's Day was just around the bend, she didn't think she'd be collecting any heartcards or sending any either. But she could see now why some people screamed and wept over the good side of love. The hateful side of love, and no one in his right mind would wish to live with those words neck-and-neck, she already had figured out with the help of the Trunk family.

Why was the couple so exposed on a balcony with only part of a shade down? The green, flat leaves on the tree beyond the balcony edge were almost floating. One branch was partially hidden behind the shade. She'd read that Japanese artists used objects in their prints to mean specific things they could not openly name. Some people looking at her print might decipher the meaning one way. Dirty Japs, she had heard people around town say for years. A lover might see it differently. What did the branch with the leaves behind a transparent shade mean? Did it mean something since the viewer couldn't see the faces of the lovers, and only the outline of the branch as it meandered out of the print, out of view?

Faceless. Cane knew that her own face was disfigured because of a birth defect, a defect that had been carried from generation to generation somewhere in the family, though her mother could never name another member so afflicted.

Cane was working her way though a book she'd discovered in her mother's shop, Modern Medical Counselor. She'd just come to "Diseases of the Skin." Cane felt if she could find a solution, a remedy, a reason for her disfigurement that some-one had overlooked, she could cure herself. There were hundreds to consider, and though the book contained color photographs, none of the swollen red and yellow crusted examples — Erysipelas, Impetigo, Favus—seem to fit Cane's facial markings. The book advised that recurring skin eruptions should be treated by a capable physician. Her doctor in Raleigh was little help. She'd tried the remedy of dogwood bark and ash an old woman had recommended to Darleen. Cane used her medicinal finger to apply it. The thumb was for the garden; the Judas finger, or the shooting finger as some called it, caused trouble; the ring finger could only heal a loved one; and the pinkie finger was for a baby to hold or suck on. So the middle finger was for doctoring. Of course, if she had a lover, a lover who would gaze at her without that look of pained uneasiness, there would be no need for other opinions or consultations on the matter.

Cane opened the secret drawer, and removed the lock box. She spun the lock right, left, right, and the metal cylinder unhooked. The print was still there. She didn't allow herself to look at it often. Yet if it had been a while, she was often convinced that it didn't really exist. She put it on her desk. She put her hand up in the air in the same position as the woman. She grasped his neck. She held her face close to his. He did not waiver. She kissed the air. She kissed his salty lips. They ate a lot of saltwater fish in his country. She grabbed her neck with her right hand. She pulled her skirt to her mid-thigh.

The doctor had assured Cane that the bumps and ruts on her face were not contagious, even the scabs.

"It's a hereditary condition. It can't be fixed, but it can't hurt anyone."

It can't hurt anyone. One time Cane had realized the man's robe was transparent and you could see through it enough to see his leg and her leg. Her leg had been placed over both of his. She was closer to him than Cane had observed at first. Her hair was pulled up into a bun that fell forward and spread out like a sea creature that had been hooked with a bone stick. Small hairs protruded at the base of her neck as if startled. And Cane could not be sure that his hand held the fan or maybe her leg held the fan while his hand was elsewhere. Cane put her leg up onto the desk. Her skirt fell back to her hip.

The idea of a man's leg and body that close to hers made the sweat on her palms gather into circles.

She looked even closer at the print. She'd missed it entirely. She took out the magnifying glass that she used to check over her photographs. With her face and the glass up close to the print without touching it, she found an outline of the man's right eye. The ink-line slanted. The pupil was black, steady. He saw with one eye open and he was looking straight at her.

Darleen Walker's Daughter
(Cane)

I never knew who my father was. I asked my mother from the get-go, but all she says is, "Cane, your father was a handsome Southern Soldier." At night she calls out to him and I sneak into her room, come up close to her ear. She taught me to be respectful and very quiet around the dead, and if I pretend she is dead, it works.

I came to her late in life and they say that's why my face is cracked, or sometimes they say it was passed along the generations. Jack Pliney told me that the word around town was that my mother slept with a dead man that wasn't all dead yet. Buckford Kent was his name. He was courting Mama, I know that much. Betsey Sunn told me he was rabid about her, said she was the sweetest mortician he had ever known. They used to go downtown and walk the square after supper.

While I'm listening to her wet lips speak some jumbled words to the Southern Soldier, I slip my hand into her jewelry drawer and find a small item to snitch. I pocket Grandma's tiny gold-and-black high school pin. She graduated from Goldsboro High in 1888. I don't have anything in my collection from her. Grandma used to tell me that in Goldsboro, she and her cousin would make a Holy Scene every December, and set it out by the road next to their farm. The first year they were having trouble getting the hay to lay down, so they used tobacco leaves their father had been drying in the barn. They couldn't remember who the three kings were, so they used scarecrows and put wreaths of grapevine on their heads since they didn't have real crowns like they do in church. They used stick figures out of dogwood for Mary and Joseph. Grandma's father had always told her that tobacco was holy and it smelled the sweetest just after it had been lit.

Grandma and her cousin grabbed a piglet from the swine shed and tied it to the manger. They lit the tobacco and sang Christmas carols until the scarecrow's arms went ablaze and the runt of the litter stopped squealing.

I never spoke to my Grandma again after she told me that holiday tale. Mama and I care for dead bodies, but I would never take part in killing a creature, even if it isn't the strongest of the bunch.

The only reason why I kept the fabric Grandma left me was that when she was young, she would go to the Carolina coast with her family and collect the wild indigo to sell to the dye-makers. The rich blue color marked the white cotton for life. I liked the story the bolt of material told. The local mill had woven only Marrow Plaid for ages, until other kinds of cotton became more popular. The material isn't available any more, except for the wintertime baby blankets I sew from my stock.

Yesterday, I made Jack Pliney help me dig up Mr. Kent's grave over at His Glory. We had to do it at night because no one understands a child's desire to know who her father is. Pliney owed me a favor since I gave him a pile of arrowheads I'd stolen from an old Paw Creek burial ground just outside of town. He doesn't know this, but I saw him go back to the burial ground and return those pointed rock spears to their graves. They were mighty fine specimens made of blue crystal, emerald, obsidian, and agate.

I'll let them be for a while.

When I used the crowbar to wedge open Buckford Kent's coffin, I thought Pliney was about to fall over dead. But he was just collecting worms that were squiggling in the soil. He's always gathering stuff like he's a scientist.

I can't tell for sure, but the jawbone of Buckford Kent sure looks like my own. Guess my mother just wanted to keep a part of him for herself through me. I felt the same; while Pliney kept sifting through rotting red clay and collecting samples for another one of his experiments with dirt, I took the jawbone.

Back at home I examined my father further. After gazing at it a while, it occurred to me who the Southern Soldier is. Down in front of the courthouse there is a tall stone statue. It is Marrow's monument to the past, Our Confederate Soldier. The soldier faces north; the marble base has inscriptions on all sides. The one legible inscription reads, "*Conquered they can never be, whose souls and whose spirits are free.*" Believe me, nobody's soul and spirit are truly free until they are dead. Even then, the family usually claims rights to anything that's left, good or bad. Or the town folk do. That soldier is crumbling to its stone bones; he's who my mother was talking about. It's easier to keep courting a stone than a dead man.

My Sister Lily
(Mercy)

"I have a secret vagina with special tunnels," my sister Lily announces to us while we're sipping iced tea and munching on hush puppies, in honor of her eighth birthday. We are eating Sunday dinner at Beebee's Fish Fry. Quiet follows her revelation as nearby eaters pause and digest the shame and embarrassment for us. Nodding and silence go a long way in Marrow, especially in public.

Beebee's serves everything but fish since we are nowhere near the coast and things tend to get rotten and stinky here if they're kept too long from the sea even in the early spring. We go out every week for Sunday dinner, even though we rarely go to church. Mother hates the church. She loves the Lord, but not his henchmen, she says. We have to dress up though, so people will think we spent the morning in the house of some Lord. Daddy rarely comes with us because this is his day to be with his family in Aberdeen.

My mother straightens her back and moves her hand with her pinkie to her neck, all the way down her stomach. That's how my little sister got into this town. She was born by Cesarean section on a Sunday. For that event Daddy did remain in town. Mama had to stay in the hospital six weeks, and when she came home they drove her to our doorstep in an ambulance.

I'm watching Lily closely to see how she's going to get out of another Look-At-Me disaster.

91

"I would show you the entrance, but I forgot the key at home," says Lily, "and anyways you all are too old to understand."

Mother decides not to respond. Her platter of BBQ has arrived with pink coleslaw and black-eyed peas bobbing in fatback juice. Poor little Lily doesn't realize how much punishment silence is. It's a good thing we're celebrating a birthday. Spring fever is in the air, so that may be to Lily's advantage, or maybe that is what made her say it. Or, maybe it is because her birthstone is aquamarine and that stands for courage according to the chart in Rose's jewelry department.

"Happy Birthday to Lily, Happy Birthday to Lily!" I mutter, between bites of a fried Chicken 'n' Innards basket. At Beebee's you get the gizzard, the heart, the liver, and the neck, too. The rest of the patrons wail along, including Mitty Hyde, Winkie Sr., and Reverend Mitchell with his Bible-raised-to-save-us, I suspect. I suspect he is about to give up. Darleen Walker, and Eunice and King Lyon, join in, so they can watch Lily, I am certain. They eye my mother too, who is dragging her fork back and forth, turning the peas into mud. People in town don't stare at me. Rather they smile almost to a laugh, as if I had been eating mustard greens and they were dangling all over my teeth without my knowledge. It's too bad Daddy isn't with us, because I try to explain these incidents to him time and time again, but he doesn't believe me. He only says the Lord works in mysterious ways and that I'm the mystery yet to be figured out. Reverend Mitchell keeps telling me I need to work harder with the Lord and that patience is a sign of purity.

But I'm going away instead of waiting. I've been sending off letters to nursing schools to see if they'll accept me. I'm the best in the health education class and my teacher says I have a knack for medical terms, so maybe I could care for the ones that are sick and dying. I'm almost 16 and I'm ready to learn some things about the world. It's all muddy here like the river; everyone knows something, but no one knows the whole thing. I'm going to study myself into intelligence and become complete.

Where we live you just have to squish around for the facts. I do know that vaginas and pee-paws are part of human anatomy. There is nothing secretive about that.

When the Spirit Moves You
(Darleen)

I started out as an undertaker's assistant. It was a strange job, especially for a female, but I needed the money and the undertaker needed me. Mr. Whitaker needed me so much I talked him into paying for my mortuary science correspondence course. And it's a good thing. He plumb fell into a coma the day after my certificate arrived in the mail. His kin let me buy the business by paycheck and I renamed it the Sweet Hereafter Funeral Home. And though people in town didn't like the idea of a female running a funeral home, they let me be because there was no one else to tend their dead.

From school I had learned how the ancients had prepared their bodies. As a tribute to them and to honor Mr. Whitaker, I prepared his body using pitch and wax. I removed his vital organs and put them in a vessel right beside his head. I painted his face with the colors of ancient Egypt, but I didn't over do it with the mascara like they did way back when. I was right proud of my accomplishment, but had learned from Mr. Whitaker the less you tell the kin about preparing, dressing and presenting the body the better. No one really wanted to know the truth. But if they had asked me out right, I would be willing to set them straight. At the viewing everyone remarked about his golden, kingly appearance. If Cane had been around then, she could have resold his likeness a hundred times over. It was magnificent if I do say so myself. As they first set eyes on him, his family thought I had mixed up Mr. Whitaker's body with another.

I, of course, would never let that happen. I am organized in a way that makes others envious. The embalming fluids I use — borax, phenol, formaldehyde — are measured in an exact way so that the body appears present with the family, until it is put underground, where it decomposes whether you like to think about it or not. I use crocus and grape dyes to make the coloring on the face and limbs as natural as possible. For the local women, I always spray them with Blue Grass Perfume, unless there is a special request. If it is someone I don't know, I use what is easiest to obtain. Rose's Department Store is generous about giving me free samples of the latest French perfumes. With the men, of course, there is but one choice, Spicy Talc. No one has ever complained or even requested another product, though I hear that up north, the new thing is to give the body a close shave, pat it down with Brut Cologne, and manicure the nails and paint them! Lord, help me. The only positive change I've read about lately is that, according to the Morticians Association Newsletter, I can call myself a Funeral Director instead of an undertaker or embalmer. I like the sound of that. Plus, they want us to start calling the coffin a casket, though it will take a bit of time for my tongue to get around that notion. I can't say it with a poker face yet, much as I've tried. But it does mean I can raise my prices.

My job is not an easy one. The floaters are the worst, the ones that have been holed up in the Tear River for days. They are so inflated, Wilbert, my assistant, is always afraid they will pop and deflate as he's moving one and the insides will gurgle out all over him. What I don't like is removing all the shellfish that has attached itself to the corpse's various openings. Mussels, shrimps, and those powerful but tiny freshwater crabs that stay alive for days, love to clamp down their claws on you, just as you think you're free of them.

I did have that man from Virginia who was still so sweet on his wife he wanted her wrapped in honey. It is a preservative, so I agreed. He wanted to honor his "Queen Bee." He bought up the honey from two farmers in the area. I knew I needed a goodly amount to cover her body, since she had been a large woman in all the ways one could imagine. Cane did notice the change in smell in the Home, because, for a day or two, the place was pleasant to sit in. Not that I mind its regular odor. I am used to it by now. I dump the bodily waste and unused embalming fluids down the sink and the fumes flow back up and just about slap you in the face. The smell of dead bodies doesn't jar my nasal passages or clog them any longer. My hands are so comfortable being around the chemicals that if a drop falls on my skin, nothing happens. Most people don't like their own nature-given smell. They shush it up with fancy fragrances and deodorant creams that leave worse stains than the ones that come from perspiration. I do not perspire, though, or have body odor that is shameful to a man. A lot of the women in this town smell, but like I said, smells on a dead body — or live one, for that matter — do not bother me.

It's other things that run me in a circle of vexation. The florist sometimes shorts me on my commission. One woman wanted her dead child to wear her haircomb with nine large gray pearls at the top, but the child had no hair. I had to jab the comb into the head of the child to get it to stay. The woman, who had wanted to watch, got all in a thither about the harm I had caused her child. Through the years I've learned it is better to keep the kin at bay when I am working.

The services I provide are fair. I've worked it out with Reverend Mitchell and the other ministers and preachers in town so things at the church or gravesite run smoothly. Each funeral gets a song at the beginning, like "Onward Christian Soldiers," a prayer, obituary reading, scripture reading, a sermon, and then the service ends with, "Lord, I'm Coming Home." The Reverend and I agree it is easier if you plan it out for the grieving family members.

I think the only time I was scared for myself was handling a Captain of the Men of the Dead body. I'd wrap myself up like a mummy for protection when preparing one of them, because often there was a little breath left in the cadaver and when you moved it the body would breathe out on you. Besides being terrified, you could end up with consumption. I told Cane a while ago that she needs to make sure I'm dead before she proceeds. Check the heart and the pulse. Wait and then repeat. The first time she practiced hearing my heart she said, "I hear a boom, Mama. I think you swallowed something backwards."

Not that Cane or I have ever had anyone come back from the dead. It did happen to a mortician in Ashville, who was about to prepare a body when it sat up, got off the table, and walked out the door. The man had a sleeping disorder that made his body slow down to zero, while his wife thought his day had come. I had to smile at the thought of that woman looking up from her kitchen sink or table as her man came back from the funeral home on his own two feet. "Sakes alive!" she'd declare and fall down dead herself from fright.

Anyway, like I said, the less you tell the family, the better. As a joke, I put a pulley-bone above Cane's shop doorway. The first young man that comes through that door will be the one she marries, or so the saying goes. She's so sensitive these days though; I'll just enjoy a private laugh about it.

"But her end is bitter as wormwood, sharp as a two-edged sword."

Miss Dunnet met her kind of death on Friday in the middle of March. That is, she made sure the graveside service was to her specifications. The minister objected to her request to serve tiny glasses of her homemade wine, but since it was the Lyon family he let it go; the Lyon's large yearly donation to his church was one of the few things he looked forward to. In addition to the special libation, Miss Dunnet had made up a guest list including mostly young people from the area, her servants and gardener, and a few adult neighbors. She specified that her son King and her husband had to arrive and leave together. In anticipation of her death, she had left King a watch with a band woven out of her hair and locks from her three dead children.

Cane was asked to attend and, since the service was to be held at night, she agreed. Mr. Lyon wanted her to photograph the event anyway. The Lyon family had donated scores of scrapbooks to the library, documenting the life and times of early Lyon members of the community. This would be another opportunity to fill a scrapbook even if Miss Dunnet's life was mostly filled with sadness. Miss Dunnet, Cane thought, had tried to live on what life had served her and it just made her weaker.

When Cane got to His Glory, there was a small crowd of people waiting outside the mausoleum. Torches had been lit at sunset. The sky looked Polynesian. Tropical. Miss Dunnet would have enjoyed that. Cane had one mourning dress of fine black silk. It had a matching black wool hat with a lace veil. It covered her face perfectly, and she could see through it without anyone seeing her face clearly. The Cuffee sisters had sent it to her just because. They tended to do quirky things like that. One day, when she was still new to the business, they had stepped into her shop. The three of them, arm in arm, proceeded to tell her the facts of life. They told her how to dye her hair if she wanted. They told her what to do if her inner skin wasn't attached. Some girls are just born that way, they said. And they told her to stay away from doctors. That was the extent of their advice. Recently, Cane heard they had sent Ulla Trunk a swimming suit for her Sweet 16 birthday.

When Jack Pliney arrived, he came over and stood near Cane. A swarm of birds flitted in and out of the oak trees above them. He cleared his throat. Not much got under Jack Pliney's skin, but the look on his face was one of discomfort. He pointed to a decaying oak that had blackberry vines coiling up the trunk. *Helmitheros vermivorus*, he said in her ear. He'd taught her the names of the local birds in Latin. His liquor-tinged breath gave Cane goose bumps. Mr. Pliney never drank. She guessed he was closer to Miss Dunnet than most folks thought. Though he could have stayed up with Mr. Lyon drinking the grief away. Some men did that. The birds were tipsy, too, while the stars and planets shined brighter against the chill of the evening.

As Cane stepped away from him she knocked into her camera, and it started to topple. A local boy, Winkie Jr., caught it and Cane grabbed his hand by mistake. In an effort to untangle herself from the warmth of his skin, she hooked her ring finger under his. The lace veil flapped and she pulled her camera tripod up between his legs by mistake. He let out a tiny yelp, a cry known only to boys and men.

"Sorry, Winkie," Cane said. She steadied her equipment and smoothed out her dress. They both noticed the slow sound her hand made moving down the silk folds, sliding, then pausing.

Winkie looked up. His corn-colored hair was slicked to the side and he'd put on his Sunday best. "Funny how those worm-eating warblers always know when to show up. Guess they find dinner whenever they can." Cane looked over at Pliney and nodded.

"Miss Walker," Winkie said, looking hard at her, trying to move the veil with his eyes. "Good evening, Miss Walker. Good evening." Winkie repeated the words as if he were unsure where the force to speak them came from.

Cane focused on his man-sized hands that stood out from his youthful body. He then moved inside with the rest of the crowd before Cane could respond. Cane saw Jack Pliney swallow a smile and she stamped her foot in his direction. "None of that from you," Cane said as they entered the Lyon family resting place. The cool metal of her camera would lower her body temperature, she hoped.

All the people packed into the small space of the Lyon Mausoleum kept Cane's mind off of her work. She thought about Mr. Tatter's pickled specimens and her own pitiful life. Cane found it hard to stay focused at funerals; her thoughts flew around like wish flowers.

Mr. Lyon spoke briefly. He had a war-torn look, though he'd never served. King was by his side, blubbering. He kept looking at his new watch. Though he was a mama's boy and some said a half-wit, King stood at attention in the shadow of his father's presence. Cane was glad she had brought her Leica as well. It was weightless and quiet. Getting the correct lighting inside was a gamble, but the almost-silent clicking avoided intrusion or attention.

After the service, everyone was expected to return to the Lyon household for a funeral supper. Cane had no intention of going to that gathering, plus she was still steadying herself from the encounter with Winkie Jr. She separated herself from the group, packed up her equipment, and gently walked towards the Tear.

"Miss Walker," Jack Pliney called out, "Mr. Lyon wanted to be sure you got a few photographs up at the house." Jack Pliney sounded so formal and foreign, Cane almost didn't recognize his voice. He walked up closer to her, and she noticed the sadness of Miss Dunnet's passing had curled his shoulders. "There will only be candlelight at the house. Mr. Lyon will notice if you don't attend." His voice had settled back into himself. She knew he was right.

Cane focused on the bounty of food crowding the dining room table. A five-layer jelly-roll cake, graham gems, snitchy pies, sweet damson pickles, and a vat of banana pudding covered one side of the Colonial era table. She clicked and flashed away as fast as she could without being impolite. Jack Pliney had been right about the lack of illumination. Cane felt protected behind her veil, until she caught sight of Winkie Jr. staring at her as he stood in the doorway to the living room. He brushed his fingertips in slow motion across his chest knowing full well that she was watching him. She turned back to the food and shook him off. Many of the mourners were filling their plates as if this were their last supper. The other half of the table was full up with chicken and dumplings, slices of Skeeter Grove smoked ham, greens laced with fat back, fire-red jello and three dishes of cucumber catsup. The highlight of the meal, and Miss Dunnet's favorite, was elevated in the center. Why she had adored roast possum with sliced sweet potatoes floating in butter was curious to Cane, but she recorded it on film as requested. She figured Miss Dunnet's comfort foods were probably too country for the Lyon clan, but in death her every wish was granted. Cane took numerous group shots and one of King's father, gazing at his son. Just before she clicked her camera, Mr. Lyon put his hand over his eyes.

River Tales

Mercy Haydon wasn't the only person in town keeping tabs on Cane Walker. What started out as an unexpected encounter for Winkie Jr., turned into a quest of discovery and desire. How, after all these years of watching the women of Marrow walk by his father's shop, he should set his mind on Cane Walker was a puzzle only the Lord could figure out. Because it made no sense to him. And maybe it was that she kept herself so hidden and it was the secrecy of her he desired, though he thought there must be more to it than that. Winkie Jr. hoped there was more to himself than that. He had known one or two other girls, but one wouldn't say he was experienced. No, he had been initiated, but there still remained a few questions about males and females he wished someone could answer. He never got that kind of detail from his buddies or strangers. His friends told him that his winking-eye trouble had to do with thinking about women all the time, but he never believed it because there were so many generations of Winkies and, anyway, he had been afflicted with the problem since birth.

After noting the times that Cane Walker left her shop and that she rarely slipped out before dark, Winkie Jr. decided he would just follow her home one day. That day arrived when he came around the corner and saw her locking up. Of course, the bank locked its doors, but other than that, Cane Walker was the only one in town who did so. More hiding, Winkie told himself.

She went home by way of the side streets and onto the dirt roads that started not too far away from Main Street. She looked pretty from behind in her plaid skirt. Her hair was glossy and pretty as if she washed it in wild grape juice. She was careful about walking near the light, any kind of light. She seemed to see it before it could shine on her. Winkie had no idea what her face looked like. He'd heard all the ugly talk and half believed it.

She headed up Elon Street towards the Tear. She broke off a peach blossom sprig. At the corner of Elon and Cardinal, Cane took three roses from Sally Hyde's mother's front yard. What was she figuring to do, wondered Winkie. And then it struck him that maybe she was meeting someone, maybe she had a beau. He halted and almost tripped over himself. It had never crossed his mind that she might be taken. Who? Who could it be? Cane was friends with so few people in town; in fact, he couldn't name one of them, except the Lyon's gardener. Cane walked on towards the banks of the Tear through an overgrown-forested section. The kids in town insisted it was haunted and called it Nobody's Land. Winkie was not deterred and followed his desire at a safe distance.

As he entered the forest he heard swirly, high-pitched sounds from the pine siskin. Usually he was adept at walking without making a creak or crack. He'd learned that skill early on in order to sneak out of his parent's house to meet his buddies. The towhees had filled up a tree and were singing, drink your tea; drink your tea, just like his mother said to his father. He almost laughed.

The forest gave way to bald clay, patches of droopy watercress, and snatches of bumpy sand between greenery. He reached down and collected a handful of cowpeas. The rush of the Tear was loud and furious. Winkie thought he had kept back far enough, and he had even removed his shoes, but the noise of his feet squishing the guinea grass turned a few creatures toward him, and Cane Walker was one of them.

For seconds the sounds of nature marked their wordless

confrontation. Cane settled into the sand and had the advantage of being low to the ground. Winkie found her because the quarter-moonlight reflecting off of the river caught her amber eyes. In one of her hands he made out the bouquet of leaves, branches and flowers. The top button of her blouse was undone.

"I didn't mean to startle you, Miss Walker."

"I don't think I was the one that was startled," said Cane, trying to get away from the reflecting water. As Winkie's eyes fluttered, Cane squirmed and dug her free hand into the sand.

Cane spoke again, lifting her grain-covered hand to her forehead, "What songs did your mother sing to you when you were a baby?" A whippoorwill flew by and they both followed its sound.

"Now that's a question," Winkie said stepping forward and then stopping himself like he'd thought better of it. "Seems like Mama only sang me one song that I can remember." He settled back into his unspoken side of the sand, trying to hide his eagerness at seeing her. "You must know it. It goes,

> *Sleep, baby, sleep*
> *Our cottage vale is deep;*
> *The little lamb is on the green,*
> *With woolly fleece so soft and clean.*
> *Sleep, baby, sleep.*

"There's another verse, but I can't recall what it is."

Cane arched her back and tipped her chin upward, and for a second Winkie thought she might stand up.

> *Sleep, baby, sleep,*
> *Down where the woodbines creep;*

Cane sang in a voice she saved for herself and the departed.

Be always like the lamb so mild,
A kind and sweet and gentle child.
Sleep, baby, sleep.

"Yes, that's it. I'd forgotten until I heard your fine voice," Winkie said. "Mama told me once that she was the only one who could get me to sleep at night."

"I hear you find sleep-comfort with the help of fermented Scuppernong."

Cane didn't know why she'd said that. Her mother drank, too, and it was only hearsay about Winkie Jr. and his crowd. Some part of her enjoyed being plain mean. Winkie Jr. was kind enough and he was old enough.

"I won't deny it, Miss Walker, I do like the taste of very ripe grapes." Winkie decided if he couldn't move closer, he could at least sit in the sand and be at the same level as Cane. "What is that you're collecting?"

Cane let the sound of the river fill up the space between them.

"There's a meaning to every plant and flower. I like to put a story together in these bouquets for some of my customers and for some of the people in town who have died. It adds to a photograph and sometimes helps the grief-stricken. This is cedar leaf, peach blossom, and Carolina roses." Cane sucked in her lips to keep herself from talking further.

"What does it mean? What's the story?" Cane didn't say anything. Winkie threw the cowpeas at her. "It's not a secret is it?" Cane bit her lips to keep from smiling.

"Starting from the outside in, I live for thee, I am your captive, love is dangerous."

"Who in town ordered that? Let me guess? Was it for Miss Hyde? No, no, it was the new school teacher, wasn't it?" Winkie was aware that as he moved the upper part of his body forward Cane moved her body in reverse, though her legs stayed in the sand, as if they were two weeping willows sway-ing, yet constrained by their trunks. "I forgot, it's for somebody who is already dead, right?"

"Not sure yet," Cane said. She decided not to tell Winkie Jr. that normally she would need to see the body first before she decided on the bouquet and that this time she wasn't thinking about a dead body when she collected the blossoms and leaves.

As they sat on the bank, the eater-bugs feasted on the juices of spring greens. Down river, Winkie and Cane could hear a boat approaching. They heard manly conversations echo off the trees and the stop-start motion of a motorboat weaving around the roots of the Tear. Winkie knew their encounter was coming to an end, but he didn't want to be the first to leave. Instead, Cane rose and shook off her skirt and as she did that, Winkie looked down her blouse and could just make out two plump breasts, the kind he'd like to lay his head on, the kind he was sure could lull him to stay awake.

"Winkie," Cane said, as she was about to leave. Winkie's eyes opened and closed nine times before he could answer.

"Yes."

"Do you think you could stop calling me Miss Walker? Call me Cane."

"OK."

A boat was approaching. Winkie suspected it was the river thieves out for a night of carousing. Winkie's father purchased a variety of items from the thieves. Winkie Sr. had a long-standing agreement with the river thieves who stole from the farms and other boats up and down the Tear River. The *Daily Gazette* had reported that a stockroom full of drug samples smuggled out of Duke University were stolen by the river thieves just last month, using old Paw Creek Indian under-ground tunnels. These ancient routes allowed them to sneak onto the campus unnoticed. Though Winkie Jr. knew Cane

Walker could take care of herself, he was glad the two of them would be moving along before the men floated by.

Cane left first. She exited by a path that followed the river a stretch before it turned off toward her house. Winkie stepped back from the sandbank after he was convinced she was safe, and hid behind a tree. As the men in the boat passed he heard them talking about how stupid educated folk were.

The waterways, underground canals and tunnels that the Indians had used to attack the British long ago, the thieves exploited now and had their run of Raleigh, Durham, and Chapel Hill.

Sweet Something

Dewey "Winkie Jr." Lamm winked all the time and couldn't help it. Most everyone in town knew about Winkie Jr.'s affliction. He was born that way. His father's name was Winkie Sr., but he was so interested in town gossip, they say Winkie Sr. never winked. The tic must have skipped a generation. Some folks said Winkie Jr. was odd because Winkie's mother came from Florida.

After Cane saw Winkie Jr. at the river, she decided that on two occasions Mr. Dewey Lamm had been winking at her in a sincere way. She made note of it in her appointment book. March 15, at 12 noon, he stuck his head in her shop, winked and then left, and just two days ago on April 2, at 6 p.m.

Today, right at closing he stepped inside her shop smelling like cough syrup and smashed grapes. Cane had lit a few candles to honor the Catholics she had photographed. It was Good Friday and Winkie Jr. and his friends used any available libation to celebrate, though Winkie Jr. wasn't Irish or Catholic. He was part trash hound and part river crab.

"Cane as sweet as —" he stopped and they both knew there was no ending to his sentence. He'd never seen her in so much light. Instead he fingered the insides of the extra-large catafalque lying on the floor. Cane had gotten it for a discount because its size made most photographers uneasy. Her mother laughed when she saw it and said it was big enough for a plague.

"Don't you tire of looking at dead bodies?" Winkie asked looking to the sides of her face as if his eyes weren't able to see clearly straight on. "You and your mama must have seen hundreds." He removed his shoes and stepped onto the black drape that covered the wooden platform.

"Come stand in here with me. I want to see your face close up."

His hand wavered and then motioned Cane to him. No one had ever wanted to see her up close. Even her doctor in Raleigh seemed to keep his distance in his starched, white uniform and with his extended, taut arms.

"Winkie Jr., you had better run along. You and I both know you're full of rotten grapes you stole from Miss Dunnet's leftovers, and those bottles of cough syrup that your Daddy gets for free from the river thieves. Those bottles are as lethal as death in this town."

As she finished her speech, she took a step closer, and Winkie grabbed onto her hands.

"They're as tender as rabbit paws," Winkie said. He started to bring them to his lips, when he straightened up and took a two-lung breath. She did look like all the pretty had been taken out of her. Winkie's mother had told him that Cane had extra feelings because of her face. It wasn't fair, but it was the way the Lord worked. Her fingers were slender, silky and her nails were neatly trimmed. He kissed them gently. He remained steady even with a drop of revulsion spinning in his stomach.

"You and I are both afflicted, Cane. We are partners in a strange way, like when there is a fire in the woods and the animals that are usually enemies, all meet up in the river for protection." Winkie Jr. tried his best not to let his eyelids bounce haywire, right at her, but he couldn't help it. It was the third time in two months, Cane noted.

"I photograph the schoolchildren when Mr. Holt can't and I make wedding portraits, too. I even took one of Jack Pliney and his wife after they got married. It's not only the dead ones that I capture."

Cane was sure the air had stopped circulating for a moment.

She took off her shoes and stepped close to him. They had a lot of room to spread out in; lying down was easy. Since it was after closing she didn't worry about anyone coming in, or her mother opening the side door from the mortuary. Her mother always left on time.

It felt funny at first to be where the dead bodies lay. They both laughed at the same time and didn't debate it further. Maybe because Winkie Jr. was more relaxed than usual, or maybe because he was so practiced in this act — or so she had heard — that Cane felt at ease and let her body drift toward him. She was in the Tear River and the rush of the water swirled around her. She saw Riley Trunk suddenly for a second and then he vanished. Winkie Jr. kissed her hard and ran his hand over the ruts on her face.

"It's softer than I expected. From a distance it looks all knotted and callused." Cane held him close. No man had ever heard the secret knocking from her heart. No man had ever laid a gentle hand on her face.

She thought about the parts of the dead men she had seen. A belly full of blubber. Piles sticking out of a worn bottom. Even Winkie's grandfather had been bald from head to toe, without a trace of white stubble. All the sex organs she had viewed seemed smaller and more medical. She had expected a vision of beauty when she first started taking photographs. Now she took little notice of body parts, except as a photographer doing her job.

But Winkie's body heated hers. He made her jolt; his movements settled into hers like layers of wet earth. Cane had ordered *Sex, Harmony, and Love* from a publishing company in New York. It had arrived in a plain brown wrapper. She had carefully read the section, "What to Allow a Lover to Do," which advised her to wait for Winkie Jr. by counting. So she did.

Winkie Jr. was slower than she expected, but Cane was amazed how his private parts grew, expanded. Her mind kept

reviewing another section in the book that said, "avoid the tor-
turing results of ignorance." So she followed the diagrams and
pictures from memory to help him along.

He called out to Jesus and a few other religious figures.
Cane too called out to someone, but she wasn't sure she was
really talking to Winkie Jr. Jack Pliney had told her that love
was like a foreign language and sometimes you just couldn't
find the right word in your own tongue to express it.

By the look on Winkie Jr.'s face, it was clear Cane had
exceeded his manly expectations. They lay there into the night
with both their eyes wide open. Cane thought of the story her
mother told her about the Ick and Wick twins. To distinguish
the dead brothers in their double casket, she'd put putty on
Ick's eyelids to keep them open. Wick's eyelids stayed closed
until moments before the viewing, so Darleen put dimes on
each lid to keep them shut. But when a mourner bumped into
the boys' coffin, one of the dimes fell off and one eye opened.
Cane felt love was like that.

Winkie Jr. got up to dress. Before he left he cupped both
his hands around her face. "Sweet as Cane, sweet as Cane," he
said.

On his way to the door, he knocked over a jawbone. He
held it in his hand and tried to see it in the dark.

"Who does this belong to?"

"Nobody I ever knew." Cane said. She tilted her face
toward him and framed a shot.

Truth Be Told
(Winkie Jr.)

Jack Pliney told me she sometimes comes by this way to the cemetery. He must have seen the urgency in my manner, a trapped animal. He must think we are the craziest people on earth, though sometimes his people do crazy things, too. I need to see her again, and it seems the only place to meet is where the dead people rest. It would be risky at her shop. Too many folks look at me when I walk near there. They surely don't know the truth, but they suspect something. Just the way the clay hitches itself to you, people see your guilt or innocence.

I'm a bird of prey, circling my own dead body for food. It's that bad. I lied to my folks. I told them I was going to drop off a prescription at the Sweet Hereafter for Cane's mother. I did do that but only so I could see if Cane was still there. I called ahead to make sure Darleen would wait. I ambled by Tillie's and tipped my hat to her. If you don't acknowledge her, she tells stories about you until you and your kin are red in the face. I stopped and looked in the window at Dapheen's Fine Jewelry Store on the square next door to the bank. She displays all remedies for marriage and love, but none that would help me, yet. My mother gave me a stack of letters to mail, so I had to drop them off and smiled at the postmaster, so he wouldn't tell my mother I was a mean sort. You have to be very careful in this town. If you pass the Fire Station late in the evening when you should be in bed, the next morning your folks and neighbors will ask you what you were doing. It is a trial to be a man in Marrow.

It's a trial to be an only child. I bear the cross of my parents and I am my own keeper. I should have left long ago, but my father needed my help in his store, or that's what my mother implied. A number of my friends have stuck around. Only three left. One works at a bank in Charlotte, and another went to college at Duke, and Lindsay Foster is playing basketball at Wake Forest but not doing so well in his studies.

Directly behind the Confederate Statue is The National Bank of Marrow. At the southwest corner of the square is the Texaco Service Station. Nearby is the funeral home and Cane's photography studio.

I like the square at dusk, when people are headed home and the buildings empty out. I met my first girl here on the square right in front of the courthouse. It was during the Harvest Festival and she was visiting her aunt. She smelled like a foreign flower I could never name. She let me kiss her goodnight, but that was it. And just on the cheek, though I held her close and felt the heat smoldering in her body.

I reached Darleen's. I walked inside and she didn't notice.

"Here's your delivery, ma'am." Darleen looked up and pointed to a coffin. I couldn't make myself call her Miss Walker because that was reserved for Cane, even though she wouldn't let me call her that anymore. I dropped the denture cleansing powder where she indicated and bid her goodnight. I looked into Cane's shop and saw no one in sight. If I hurried I was sure I could find her at His Glory.

I took the Catholic route to the cemetery. There were so many paths to His Glory, religious and otherwise. The Paw Creek Indian trail runs wide through the middle of His Glory. It was here a good 200 years before every other trail. The Methodist path is skinny and neat. I still went to the Methodist Church with my parents because it was important to them. I didn't mind the words in the Bible, it was how the minister expressed them to me that gave me cause to grumble. I don't need to be reminded again and again how I have failed, how I have sinned, how much I need the minister to show me the way to salvation.

I caught a glimpse of her bending down at a mound of dirt. I could have sworn she was singing. It seemed like there were lights shooting up from the graves. If I had believed Granny Ma'am's chatter, she would have called them witches' eyes.

As if Cane could read my mind, she looked in my direction. I was struck by the way her delicate hand beckoned, how her fingers curled at her heart. I'd seen her in more light and I knew the geography of her face. It looked so much worse than it felt.

As I reached her, I saw sparks shoot out of the older graves.

"It's the dancing souls of children," Cane said. And I believed her. One of the few comments my mother had ever made about Cane was that she was born an edge-child, half in this world and half in the other. Mother had said it with sadness in her voice, not for Cane, but for herself.

Cane had made a space for us. "They are at peace now, Winkie."

I lay down with her right there in the dirt. I couldn't not lay down. It wasn't right I know to lust, to love so close to the dead, to love this girl without wedding her first. We were side by side talking in sounds that make sense only to lovers.

We had gotten each other just to a point of sizzling frustration when we heard a female voice call out. Cane was sure it was Mercy Haydon. I suspected it was Darleen but didn't dare say it. In silence we untangled from one another. We had to escape before we were found out or had time to finish. To be safe we took the overgrown Primitive Baptist route out.

Lessons of Chance

Mercy and her friends sat around July 4th and showed each other the insides of their vaginas. Miss Raleigh-Lolly as they called Eunice behind her back, had a huge birthmark, like a piece of liver. She cried and cried while showing it to them, since she was sure her boyfriends, of whom she had none yet, would think her used and pearly.

"It's bad enough when your time of the month starts," Eunice said to Mercy and Ulla, waiting to see if they knew about such things.

Mercy's mother had told her early on about how the body of a girl works. Mercy had asked her mother about the body of a boy, but Grace put her off, telling her she'd talk about that part of growing up when she got a little older. Everything in pieces, always half-done, Mercy had thought.

Ulla already knew about ladies from her mother and about men from her father, so nothing Eunice referred or alluded to surprised Ulla. Not much was left for Ulla to be surprised about, though her father had stopped touching her down there for now, and that was unexpected.

"It's just an inside birth mark, not any different than the beauty mark Ina Ladder has on her cheek. And everyone admires that," Mercy said.

Ulla nodded. "Think of it as your private beauty mark," Ulla said, but they all knew there was something strange, sinful, and smelly about it, and though Mercy and Ulla wished they had the Lyon money, they didn't want Eunice Lyon's mark.

"Does it stink?" Mercy asked. She'd smelled herself before and one time her mother smelled like wet clay. Eunice shook her head.

"Mine's pretty narrow, I can hardly see it." Mercy said. The color of her vagina was pink like doll lips.

Ulla's vagina was wide as a gash and she showed it to them briefly hoping they wouldn't see what she only knew.

"I'll never find a husband," Eunice said. She closed her labia like a book and pulled up her frilled underpants. She sucked at her fingers and wiped them off with her cotton slip. The smocking design on her dress was of Mary and her little lambs. "She tries to keep me from growing up," Eunice said about her childlike attire. Her mother bought all Eunice's clothes at Ellis Stone's in Durham. Eunice had dresses for every occasion. Her mother had even bought her a sweet sixteen dress, but Eunice was sure there wasn't an outfit anywhere that could completely hide the mark that existed in-between her legs.

"I guess I could bleach it. My mother puts bleach above her upper lip to keep black hairs blonde, but they grow back black at a startling speed, like they're in a race that they always know they'll win. At least I don't have the same problem as Cane Walker."

The other girls agreed. Mercy recalled a saying her mother had told her the first time she made fun of Cane Walker.

> Beauty is skin deep
> Ugly to the bone
> Beauty will fade
> Ugly will hold its own.

She didn't mention it to her friends because she didn't know if it applied to Cane or Eunice.

The Ballad of the Cuffee Sisters

For a long spell the townspeople of Marrow ambled on, sipping sodas and sunning themselves around the town square. The limestone courthouse sank a bit more, and even a few people started to notice. Another limb of the war statue crumbled away to the stone bone and broke off right in the middle of the day. The townsfolk didn't know quite what to do about that, so they did nothing and said less. The Silver Queen corn was beyond its peak, mealy and bug-ridden. The tomatoes were overproducing so much that most folks set out a pail of them for free in their front yards. Betsey Sunn said when she was a child, tomatoes were called poison apples and no one ate them; they just put them in a bowl for decoration until they molded. They were molding today, too.

Cane Walker was showing a belly that she hid underneath her photographer's coat, and if anyone suspected that she was pregnant, not one person had mentioned it. The summer peaches were lush and fleshy, better than the ones from Georgia. Mitty Hyde had spied Cane sitting in front of her shop one evening. Cane ate nine fat ones in a row like it was a private contest. The juice rivered around the scars on her face and Mitty saw her suck at each pit until it was clear of pulp. As she approached the Sweet Hereafter Funeral Home, Mitty formed the intention to say something about Cane's unwomanly appetite to Darleen. Three clear howls rang out, evenly spaced. They were guttural, primitive tones, but pure. Cane jerked her head in the direction of the sound and knew right away it was coming from the Cuffee sisters at the corner of Lincoln and Elon.

"Better get your mother," Mitty said to Cane. "I'll get after Sheriff Hayes." Cane hesitated a moment. The Cuffee sisters had been a vocal topic lately. Tullah, Eullah, and Buellah had stopped paying their taxes years ago. They said they'd given enough to their country and state. Lord knows they gave their hearts to the circus. Their home was overrun with paper, old cans, trunks from all their travels with the circus, spider webs that they had dusted with glitter, and three sets of rocking chairs in the living room, kitchen, and the one bedroom they all shared now, the two other bedrooms being filled up with their past, as they told the county officials. The porch also had a set of rockers painted with symbols no one could decipher. Winkie Sr. insisted they were old Freemason symbols, but Cane and Jack Pliney thought they were Paw Creek Indian markings. Just last week the county authorities had given the Cuffees notice that they needed to vacate their home and settle into the Marrow County Home for the Elderly. It was worse than the pitchin' place in Raleigh where the unwanted children ran around with their underwear dragging in the dusty clay.

Cane held her belly as she got up and adjusted her coat. She stepped over to her mother's business and pushed the door open and went inside.

"Did you hear the noise?" Cane looked at her mother and saw that she had her embalming bag packed to go over to the Cuffee sisters' home. Darleen had a sixth sense about death and seemed to be ready to view a dead body even before it was dead. Cane doubted that her mother would ever notice she might be with child. Darleen was so fascinated with approaching death that she was unable to see budding life.

"Knew it wouldn't be long," Darleen said. "I'll need your help with this one, Cane." If her mother had noticed Cane's protruding belly, she'd kept that information to herself. For once.

Cane hadn't assisted her mother since she prepared old man Tatter's body and the two lady friends. But the Cuffee sisters had been kind to her. Once they gave her an amber necklace that had come all the way from Red Russia. For her sweet sixteen they dropped off a barrette surrounded with seed pearls and inlaid with shell. Abalone was the beauty of the sea shimmering in the palm of her hand. At night she would pull her hair back with the barrette, imagining a different life than the one she woke up to each day. And the funeral outfit with the veil hat they had sent to her New Year's Day had been a lifesaver.

Of course, Reverend Mitchell would be there in short order, and Cane was sure he'd be able to tell about the baby. He'd dropped by her house one day, pleading with her mother to bring Cane to church for a 'healing'. She buttoned her coat to the double button at the top, and she and her mother took the side streets over to the Cuffees'.

The three sisters had come to Marrow with a traveling circus in 1893. The circus needed water for the animals and the workers, so the town fathers let them set up on the eastern portion of the cemetery, near the Tear River, in a section that wasn't expected to be used for a long time. Though some folks at the time thought it was strange to mix a circus with the dead, by the time the show was all setup, no one gave it another thought. Most folks had lost someone close in town, so a trip to the cemetery with the circus side-by-side made sense.

The circus consisted of a small merry-go-round, a center ring that was tented, where the Cuffee sisters performed nightly, and a row of incredible and unbelievable caged creatures like the Mermaid with a Beard who only spoke in sea sounds, the Blind Black Bear with a paw growing out of its stomach, and Two-headed Tina, who was only three feet tall.

The Cuffee sisters had a bull they used in their act, The Bull-Fighting Banditas. They dressed up in black pants, pearl-beaded jackets, and hats that were molded to look like horns, each one covered with glass beads that sparkled in the light. "We weren't Mexican, we just wished we were somebody other than who we really were," they had told Cane once.

After performing in Marrow for weeks, the circus went bust and the owners left Marrow abruptly one night during hurricane season in a Winkie Jr. blink of an eye. It had rained so ferociously during the day that the land in the cemetery turned to drippy mud. The carousel sank further and further into the earth, while the remaining circus employees scattered with their acts and equipment in the rain-soaked hours before dawn. Only the Cuffee sisters stayed behind.

Cane and Darleen arrived at the home before Mitty and the sheriff. The porch was sagging on the left side and there were red Christmas lights dangling in the front window. Cane didn't want to enter. Her mother marched ahead pulling tightly at Cane's arm. The adventure of death never ended for Darleen. As they stepped into the front parlor, they saw the three women all together in a lump on the rug of the living room. They had tied themselves together. The smell of lavender walnut dye they all used to keep the gray and white hairs at bay permeated the room. They were wearing their Sunday outfits. The sisters had slashed each other across the face and neck, and when they fell, they settled onto one another like layers of dirt. A note on the table had four words scribbled on it: *We ain't the sinners.* Cane had to agree.

"What a mess," Darleen said. "Their faces look worse than yours, Cane."

Fruits of Labor and Love

The biggest news in the *Daily Gazette* for the next week was the Cuffee sisters' death and the unyielding heat. Mixed together with the humidity and the lack of a breeze, the town of Marrow seemed infected. Vegetable and fruit gardens were weighted down with so much produce, it was as if the earth was trying to rid itself of something: peaches, cucumbers, and heaps of tomatoes. They thrived in such conditions when flowers and humans wilted. Lily Haydon had decided to collect the pails of excess tomatoes and put them into buckets in her wagon. She walked through the streets of town singing her version of a song she'd heard Nellie and Minish sing when they were selling fruit earlier in summer.

> *Tomatoes, fresh and fine*
> *Juicy tomatoes, Ma'am,*
> *So fresh this time.*
> *Three baskets for a dime,*
> *Sweet tomatoes, Ma'am*
> *My fresh tomatoes.*

She sang her bird-heart out like she was on her way to the poorhouse and still no one would buy. It could have been the heat that kept everyone silent and uncooperative. Back and forth Lily walked through the streets, down Elon, past Fig, over to Jefferson and then along Lyon Street. Finally, Darleen Walker stepped out onto her porch. Lily rolled her wagon down the stone path to the edge of the porch steps.

"Lily Haydon," Darleen said, "didn't anyone tell you that no one wants those poison apples, especially this year?" She took a long sip of her tea while Lily noticed the skin beads around Darleen's neck. Poke outs. Some were tobacco brown, some were clay red. A few were flesh pink. One of them had a drop of sweat hanging from it.

"When I was growing up, a young lady like yourself had her mind set on other things like finding a beau and looking for love knots." Cane came up to the screen door.

"Mother, Lily doesn't know about stuff like that. She's..." Cane paused, "she's just a child."

"Lily, how many baskets you got there?" Cane asked.

"I guess there are 21, two nines and one three, but the last one is smashed a bit; I won't charge you for it, if you take them all."

"Sakes alive, Cane. What will you do with that tomato mess?" Darleen said, stepping aside so she could see both Lily and Cane at the same time. As Darleen did this, the sweat bead dropped onto the porch.

"Here's two dollars, Lily," Cane said. Lily hesitated and then ascended the six steps. As she reached the screen door, it opened and Cane's hand slipped out with the bills. She didn't see much of Cane's face. The zigzag in the screen made it hard to get a good look at her, but she did notice that Cane no longer looked like an older girl, like her sister. She looked like a woman. Like her mother or like Mitty Hyde.

"You can leave them on the porch." Lily pushed her face into the screen. She whispered, "Bend a dogwood leaf over your thumb and forefinger. If your sweetheart loves you, it will pop off."

"So, Miss Lily Haydon, " Darleen said, moving closer to her as Lily went up and down the stairs carrying the baskets of tomatoes. "You should drop by more often. We don't know you as well as we know Mercy and your mother."

Cane let the screen door slam shut. As Lily patted the dollars she'd shoved into her pedal-pusher pocket, she looked up at Darleen.

"I have to be going," Lily said. "No disrespect, ma'am, but I'm allergic to morticians." Lily smiled at Cane. She jumped from the top step to the stone walk and then rolled her empty wagon as fast as her growing limbs allowed her.

> *Tomatoes, fresh and fine*
> *My fresh tomatoes, ma'am*
> *All sold out this time*

Darleen watched the Haydon girl sing her way home. She shook her head and turned in Cane's direction.

"Just what do you intend to do?"

Cane opened the door with her foot and moved it back and forth like a fan. "I'm planning to put up tomatoes and make a batch of sauce. I saw a recipe for tomato jelly and tomato cough drops."

Lily Haydon is a strange girl, Cane thought, though she had memorized Lily's unsolicited advice.

Darleen just stared at her daughter. "I don't know what you're fattening yourself up for. Prince Charming doesn't live in this town and your name isn't Cinderella. Mitty Hyde told me you were eating up a storm of peaches the other day. I guess you're just looking for Jack Sprat, now, eh?" Darleen stepped forward toward the screen and then stood back.

"If you really want to, you can go round to Rose's and get yourself a new outfit." Though Cane would never venture into Rose's, even though they were open late one night a week, she cherished the moment, the idea that her mother considered that she might want to look better than the hand-me-down and dead-girl clothes Darleen offered her.

The Trumpet Sounds Within Her Soul

Her father had said it was just a noble attempt by Reverend Mitchell to get her, Lily, and her mother back to church. Why Reverend Mitchell had decided two years ago that Mercy was the one to focus on, she never knew. Fifteen little red records had come in the book, *Golden Moments for Family Devotions*. The inside flap claimed one of the benefits of listening to the recordings was to help prevent delinquency. The Reverend had stopped Mercy on her way home from Rose's Department Store. She had been looking at herself in the mirror. Had he guessed? Did vanity cause delinquency?

Mercy had stood still and tried to keep her breathing to a minimum. Reverend Mitchell had handed her the packet of records and encouraged her to listen to each 45 again and again. "The power of the Lord's words will show you the direction." Touching her shoulder with his pale hand he added, "and even the ones who have strayed are supposed to return. It's God's will."

Mercy tilted her head in agreement and kept her breath in her throat.

"Now I am counting on you, Mercy Palmer Haydon, to show your family the way back into God's fold."

He had cornered her by putting his formless body in front of her in a way that didn't allow her to move around him.

"I know your father comes when he is not busy with his kin in Aberdeen, but you have to be the light for your mother and sister. Listen to 'Man's Greatest Contribution', that side will help you help others."

Some days it seemed to Mercy that everyone she knew had strayed.

But she was on a discovery quest to find out more about Cane Walker, who came from a whole family of strays. The older people in town spoke kindly of her, while Mercy's friends talked mean about her face and the whereabouts of her father. But no one seemed to know any facts. After the class photo session at Cane's shop, Mercy was sure she was dating Tommy West. She'd observed their interaction. A lover's spat between her classmate and that older Cane girl. It did not make any sense. But if she was going to be successful in nursing school, she had to fine-tune her observation abilities.

Cane's name didn't connect one dot with her looks. Her mother had told Mercy she imagined that Darleen named her Cane because as a child all the kids in Marrow would search out the cane fields and sneak off with some to chew on. Darleen could be seen sucking on sugarcane all day long. She had lost her teeth from eating so much. They had turned tar black before they fell out.

Mercy left the library early and walked through town around the Confederate Soldier, looking for Cane. The blue sky was switching to copper color, and she knew she would be able to find Cane, just like all the other night creatures, if she was patient. But she didn't have much time before she was expected home for dinner.

First, she prowled by Cane's house to see if she could look inside and see who was there. Darleen was on the porch, but the rest of the house was a frame without a picture. She headed to the Tear and took the path from Cane's house to the cemetery. Along the way she got bitten by a swarm of mosquitoes; she had to paddle her way out. She took in a deep breath as if she could track her scent. All people had a scent. But there was no sign or scent of Cane. Mercy figured if she really found her, she might just go up to her and ask her all the questions she had been collecting for years. Her father had told her she should face the truth head-on, because otherwise it just festered like an infected boil. Mercy was sure she'd be treating a lot of those in nursing school. Puncture, drain, and dress. That would be the healthy procedure.

She entered His Glory with little light to help her get around. As she had done for years, she walked over to the well and rubbed the sparking rock for luck. It was a tradition, though she didn't believe it would do any good. Her father had told her that when he came to Marrow, he'd heard that widows would rub the rock and look around with their glad eyes to let the men in town know they were ready to stop wearing black.

There was a fly swatter on the ground nearby. Mercy didn't have to pick it up to know it was from Darleen Walker. In the summertime they were handed out as part of Darleen's funeral package. Fly swatters that advertised Darleen's business.

Mercy brushed her fingertips over a large marble angel at an old grave. Light faded on the edges of its wings. One year when it had snowed in Marrow, Mercy and her father had made Snow Angels. They flapped their arms hard and laughed at the impressions they made in the earth. Ina Ladder had come out of her home and called to them to collect some of the snow before it melted. "Make snow ice cream!" she had said.

Mercy's mother had come out to see what all the commotion was. With her belly full of Lily-to-be, she brought them a pan and together they scooped up enough snow for the three of them. Adding sugar, vanilla extract and milk they whipped together the concoction and stuck it in the freezer. After dinner the three of them savored eating it. Just the three of them.

As Mercy turned away from the angel, she heard the noise. It came from the eastern section, where the newer graves were, away from the town founders and rich families. That section mingled with the circus relics and the Catholics. It was where the new people in town were buried, or the ones that had no history to get them into the older section. She slowed down and then moved forward carefully. The cemetery had never scared her; she had thought of it only as a playground instead of a death-ground.

At first she heard what she thought was moaning, a couple possibly visiting a deceased family member. Had they come from far away to visit? Most people she knew came to His Glory on Sunday afternoon to pay their respects. Otherwise, it was empty throughout the week, except for kids and Cane Walker.

She let herself move a bit closer. Out of respect she didn't want to be seen or see their grief. The wails were growing and subsiding and then growing. She got close enough to make the outline of two people prostrate on the ground. Were they on top of a grave? Were they on top of each other? She reared her head with awareness of the act between a man and a woman. She hovered like a gnat. It was awkward, the motion she could hear and almost feel, the pressure of the two bodies moving like the rhythm of a circus ride. *Sin-sick-souls.*

"Eunice!" she shouted into the growing blackness.

The noise stopped. The couple moved with such agility, Mercy thought they might have been animals. They knew their way around the cemetery. She had not heard words, just utterances. Maybe one of the Skeeter Grove boys had captured one of her classmates. But she didn't hear a girl crying or struggling. Maybe he would come and get her. Maybe he was a murderer.

"Yea, though I walk through the shadow of the valley of death, I will fear no evil."

Mercy said this over and over to herself as she left the cemetery, softly stepping over graves. She had just played one of her records that morning, "Be Not Anxious." She'd keep on her journey to corner Cane and ask her personal questions, but she'd do it by daylight or with Ulla by her side.

Winkie's Cup of Love

Since people in town rarely looked at her straight on, it wasn't hard to hide it. Winkie Jr. was a witness, a participant, and struggled to accept it in his mind, though he left Cane care packages at the shop while she was next door at her mother's. Or sometimes, he'd slip by first thing in the morning, since Cane was arriving later than usual. He'd leave some offering, some gesture of knowing: Planter's Benedicta Tablets, Dr. Caldwell's Syrup Pepsin, or smelly 666 liquid that was suppose to somehow help females. Cane suspected they were free samples from his daddy's shop.

Cane always shook her head after finding the gifts. She knew you had to be very clever if you were going to steal, and she thought Winkie Jr. was being careless. Not that she would ever say a word or cast a stone.

These days Winkie's eyelids were opening and closing at a clipped pace. It was so bad that most folks in town stopped calling him by his pet name and returned to his God-given name of Dewey. Even looking at him was a trial. Family and secrets did that. His father owned the only drug store in Marrow, or as the teenagers in town called it, Winkie's Cup of Gossip. Winkie Sr. knew the insides of most families' business, or would barter to find out. It figured, though, that he didn't have a clue about his son and his budding involvement with Cane. It's just like preacher's kids and rich folks. They always sin the worst and hide it the best, at least from their parents. Or they try to.

On Wednesday, Mr. Lyon's son, King, skipped by just as Winkie deposited a bunch of flowers at Cane's doorstep.

Winkie tried to disguise his intentions. King was carrying a Coke cleanser for his mama, a cola with a splash of ammonia in it. Though Miss Dunnet had died, King still went downtown to fetch a coke every day. King's mama had told Winkie it was the best healer she knew of, better than Pluto Water or Jesus. Though close to Winkie in age, King had always remained childlike. He wasn't dumb; he just never progressed to being a grown man, though he was an expert when it came to recalling names — street names and family names. Winkie let King chatter away.

"One time I spilled the cleanser on my shirt, and it tore a hole right through it," King said like a puffed-up wild turkey. "My mama had a powerful stomach."

King stopped to check himself. He looked at his watch with the human-hair band. "Those flowers for someone?"

Winkie nodded in a manner that could mean yes or no.

They both looked down at the bouquet. Winkie had chosen them special for Cane. He'd gone to the library to learn their meaning before he went picking. He was sure Cane had read *The American Girls Handy Book*. When he asked the librarian what she had read as a young lady that was her answer. He put together a whole sentence with white clover, blue violet and lemon blossom: I promise faithfulness, discretion. He circled the bouquet in white roses, to let Cane know he'd keep silent about their secret. A small arrowhead was tied to the flowers. Winkie Jr. had marked a message in clay ink: To My Sweet As Cane Girl.

"Somebody die?" King asked.

"Yeah," Winkie Jr. said, "a relative of ours from Goldsboro. Cane's mother is doing the body. I told my daddy I'd drop off some flowers for the coffin." King winked at Winkie. And then winked again. "How come your eyelids flap so much?"

King waited for an answer. Winkie tried to freeze his eyelids, but he couldn't control them, or much else these days. King stared a moment longer.

"We had catfish fresh out of the lake and hush puppies for dinner," King said.

His ears looked like the seashells Tillie sold at her store. Winkie Jr. smiled and held his fingers to his eyelids. Even that didn't help.

"Well, my Mama's spirit will be missing me," King said. He trotted off, keeping a close watch on the cola he was holding. Winkie Jr. knew from his father that Miss Dunnet had always been able to tell if King, or anybody else, had spilled a bit, or taken a sip of her drink. King managed for the most part to keep his mama's wish alive even though she wasn't.

Winkie made himself breathe.

He left the offering for Cane. He knew she would return soon and that she'd get his message. That's how they talked these days. Through objects and fingers and eye twitches. He knew he couldn't see her face to face at her shop right now. He wouldn't be able to keep from touching her again. He also couldn't stretch his mind around the idea or the fact of the child. His child. Theirs. After he had left His Glory that time with Cane, he had gone home and rocked himself to sleep, pretending their pliable limbs were still tangled.

Love Thy Father

"I don't mind so much," Ulla said, as she showed the flowers to Mercy. "I just wish he wouldn't steal them from Miss Walker, or the cemetery, for my birthday."

Ulla's hair was pulled back in two braids that met as one down her back. She was tall for her age, but she bent over a bit as if to hide from people. Mercy was always telling her to straighten up, to be as tall as she was growing.

"Cane's mother can get flowers whenever she wants, and Cane Walker is a thief, I hear, but you should still return these," Mercy said.

Ulla had wanted to but couldn't bring herself to let go of the flowers yet. She'd found the tiny arrowhead tied to the middle of the bunch. *To my Sweet as Cane girl*. How could Cane have a boyfriend? And who would want her? Who would want me? Ulla liked to imagine that some boy had given her the flowers.

"Yes, I'm going to after I fix dinner for my father. Wanna help? Daddy is up country for the day and will be home late."

Ulla meant to tell Mercy about the love note. She had to admit she wanted to hold onto it a little longer. Ulla liked the idea that she knew more than Mercy, about a lot of things. Mercy was heading out of town soon, to nursing school. She wouldn't be interested in Ulla much longer, or even Marrow. Mercy, Ulla had always thought, needed to leave in order to fill some hole in her heart. Ulla's mother had told her long ago that Mercy Haydon had an emptiness inside of her that would never be filled. Mercy wanted the world to be perfect, she wanted to be an only child and for her parents to be in love with each other. She wanted the whole town to be what it wasn't. Ulla had told her about her father and Cane at their farm a while ago. That was all Mercy could stomach. Seems like the smarty girls don't always like the truth.

"Nope. Lily needs help with her homework, so I have to go soon," Mercy said, "but don't forget about the flowers. It's not right to keep them."

Truth be told, Marrow wasn't so different than anywhere else, it just seemed that way since Mercy had never gone any-where. Neither had Ulla, but she knew other reasons that made it so. The last thing her mother had said to her was "try to love thy father." Ulla was sure she had meant the Lord, but Reverend Mitchell had told her Miss Rachel was trying to get her to obey her own flesh-and-blood father.

"Ulla, your mama wanted you to obey your closest kin." He'd said this during his weekly visits after her mother died. Ulla had had to endure the Reverend's company for a year. He would come after church services on Sunday, and after he had been to the cemetery to pay his respects. It never failed that, every time he came, he would step into her home and leave bits of red clay on her floor. If there had been a funeral service, she would know whose dirt he was carrying before he arrived. One time it was Mr. Clover; another time Reverend Mitchell stepped into the house with the Cuffee sisters' dirt on his shoes. What Ulla remembered most about their death was that Tullah, Eullah and Buellah had used three circus knives and left a short, bloody note.

After all the things Ulla's father had done to her mother, and to her, she had to believe that her mother was talking about God or Jesus, or that she died crazy.

Ulla surprised herself and Mercy by hugging her before they parted ways.

Remains

Cane sifted through the personal items of the dead, which her mother threw in the yard behind their shops. Rumors flew around town that the county officials were going to investigate complaints about missing items in the coffins and urns. Cane didn't understand the reference to urns. No one she knew was ever cremated except Mr. White, though Darleen kept a batch around just in case there was a need. After the Cuffee incident, Cane wanted to be ahead of the trouble. Usually it was a sweetheart note, an old photograph, or an empty box of candy, the contents of which Darleen had digested without one thought for the deceased. Cane gathered up what she could, reading and touching the woe and heartache. Mr. Tatter had gone to the grave without his love notes to one of the Cuffee sisters. Seemed Tullah returned every one of them, unread. The packet had fallen between Henry White's cracked urn that never made it to His Glory and a half-empty can of face powder. When Cane lifted the letters, freed them, bits of bone fell from the pages and a white dust covered her clothing like silt. She was a thief, too, she reminded herself. But at least she was trying not to be anymore. Her mother could be so sloppy with the possessions of others. But it did no good to argue with her. Darleen Walker was set in her ways, molded to them as if she feared someone or something would come into Marrow and wrench her free and make her more alone than she already was. Darleen claimed she was independent. Just an independent spear-it, she'd say. Cane thought everyone was about as independent as a puppy on ice.

Yesterday, Cane had followed her mother on her night walks around Marrow. Earlier that day, Darleen had received a package from the federal government. From where Cane stood, it looked like a mess of official documents that had 'denied' stamped on them. Darleen had talked in her sleep about getting money from Buckford's relatives, but Cane didn't know for sure what the papers meant. Darleen set out after the sun had been covered with a haze and sauntered down the trail between town and her home. The trail led to the Tear. At a clearing near the water, Darleen set the papers ablaze, the flames casting a Scuppernong light against the murky river. With the trees aglow in their autumnal brilliance, Cane had to look away, not from worry of being seen, but from fear of the kind of light being shed. Heartache light. The kind of light that burned its beauty and left nothing in its path, like falling stars or hurricane lightning.

Just as her mother was finishing her business, one of the colored families rowed a body down the river to the cemetery. It was on a wooden barge and the members of the family held the body still as the current nudged them from side to side. They prepared their own bodies in Coloredtown, but because their land was slowly falling into the Tear, they buried their dead in His Glory for a fee that made each family in Coloredtown strive hard to stay healthy and live long.

Though technically a part of Marrow, Coloredtown had been what it was for years. In fact, Betsey Sunn remembered her mother referring to it right after the Confederate War ended. Of course, there were still colored folks who lived on this side of Marrow, like Nellie and Minish and their families over at the Lyons'. But you couldn't say they had their own home or land. They were free to come and go, of course, but Mr. Lyon always made it clear who had the money and who needed it. But he did that with everyone.

As the death boat had passed Darleen, she stopped and

bowed her head. The tradition of burials brought out an automatic response in her. She'd told Cane long ago, she was glad the coloreds kept their bodies to themselves. One time Miss Dunnet begged Darleen to prepare the body of her old wet-nurse, and Darleen claimed it almost killed her, though Cane always remembered her mother as the picture of health. Sickness of any kind never touched Darleen.

Cane had neglected to tell her mother that she had on occasion taken a few pictures of dead babies in Coloredtown. Jack Pliney had asked her special and asked her not to mention it to anyone. She'd taken her portable equipment across the river, and it had all proceeded without trouble. The sister of one of the dead babies she'd photographed had come up to her and had asked Cane why her face was inside out, but other than that the day was not memorable. After the colored girl spoke to Cane, Cane had seen Jack Pliney reach over and pinch the girl on her arm in a way that the girl would remember for days.

Twelve Bites to Heaven
(Rolland)

Biscuits here, she claimed, were like the Stations of the Cross. There were 12 stops or ways to order them. If you ordered them all at once — plain; with gravy; buttered; buttered with ham; buttered with bacon; buttered with sausage; buttered with cheese and all the meats; buttered with egg, cheese, and all the meats; filled with greens; sugared; smothered in syrup; or with a side of applesauce — you were a shoo-in for heaven, or that was what people said. Or at least that was what the Grill owners wanted their customers to believe. Grace said the only shoo-in for heaven was God Himself and that was only because He created it. I knew it was sacrilegious to say so, but that was Grace Palmer for you. We first met at the P & Q Grill. I asked her what was good, and we ended up talking about religion and biscuits. A few weeks later, we got married.

I'd seen her from a distance when I walked in. She was twisting around on her counter stool, twirling her skirt. And she stopped just long enough to let me squeeze into the seat next to her. I was visiting Marrow on family business. That is, I was tracking down the history of a lost relative. "Lost" meaning no one in the family would tell me much about him, so I figured his story must be especially important. And it was, almost unbelievable. Mother just kept changing the subject when I tried to get her to tell me about him. All I knew was that there were a few Catholics on our side of the family, though the Presbyterian contingent would barely admit it. Uncle Tuba, as he was called for his sea-deep voice, was Catholic and had come to Marrow long before I was born. His Christian name was Raymond Rutherford Rolland Haydon. I was named after him. His mama had called him Triple R, until later when, I had learned, she had changed it to Triple Trouble, though for years no one would reveal to me what the multi-trouble was.

I discovered he had married a 71-year-old widow. He was 46. That was the first trouble. She was Catholic. That was the second trouble, since the family was trying to breed out Catholicism. Uncle Tuba and the widow spent a lot of time at the church, and when they weren't worshipping, Uncle Tuba was fishing off the coast of South Carolina near Myrtle Beach. The widow paid for his trips to the coast, not knowing exactly what he was fishing for. He met a young fisherman there and they spent much too much time together. That was the third trouble. The kind that happens when men only have each other to set their minds on.

I just recorded the facts in my family tree. I am the family historian. No on else wanted the job. As I told Grace Palmer that day, the truth doesn't harm me, but trying to get to it can. Though I, too, have lied, deceived myself into believing one thing when the God-given truth was something else. Mother found out what I knew, and she said I must close the book on the family history and get another job, or a wife. So I chose the latter and still kept collecting family facts.

After Grace Palmer and I chatted and stuffed ourselves with biscuits, she took me and her wiggling skirt over to the Catholic Church. It was a miniature church overrun with ivy — a forgotten castle. It was also a storage room for an old circus.

I got my jacket hooked on the animal cage entrance and Grace helped free me. The church was vacant inside. I had wanted to see where my uncle and aunt had worshipped. I was hoping to find the priest, who had known them, but he was long dead, Grace told me. I lit a candle for them, though I guess my uncle was securely ensconced in purgatory. Mutual caressing, as they once called it in England, between men was a long-standing sin.

Grace suggested we try to find their grave markers. She said the Catholic section was very intimate and it would be easy to locate. She took me right to the graves. My aunt had died first, but it wasn't long after that Uncle Tuba succumbed. I was told by my mother that no one showed up for his graveside funeral. Grace said when she was young, she and her friend Ben would come to the cemetery on Christmas Eve. One time she had seen a man, not from Marrow, drop a bunch of cornflowers on one of the Catholic graves. After he had departed, she and Ben snuck over to see who she was. They never spoke about it, but Grace remembered the name — R.R.R. Haydon — assuming, at the time, the grave was for a girl.

I stayed longer in Marrow than I meant to. Betsey Sunn had known my uncle and aunt and filled me in on some family details no one else cared to recall. I stayed on also to court Grace. She liked me, I know. She liked the idea that I was from somewhere else. That I had traveled to other places in the world, thanks to Uncle Sam. I wasn't sure I had a place in Marrow, but my uncle had found one, and Grace said she would find one for me. I told her I would have to spend a lot of time with my mother in Aberdeen, especially around the religious holidays and on Sundays. She had said she was set in her ways on the holidays, too, and didn't mind that I had my own plans with my family and the Lord.

I knew that she and Benjamin Ladder were childhood sweethearts, but while we were courting she hardly mentioned him. It was like she was trying to escape from herself. I encouraged her for my sake. When she first went with me to meet my parents, she spoke constantly and on so many topics, my mother got up and left the room. My mother never liked talky women. Grace outdid herself; she was an unexpected storm, just like the torrential rains that have poured down on Marrow this past May. The town was just about flooded into obscurity. The power and the awe of such an event of nature humbles me.

We have two children, Mercy and Lily. They are the split of their mother. They didn't take after the Haydon side. Right after Grace and I married, Benjamin proposed to Ina Lansbury. It was when Benjamin married that Grace shifted away from me. We live next door to Benjamin Ladder and his wife Ina, and I never thought a thing against it. I have been told that our marriages got mixed up, that I should have married Ina, and let Grace find her way back to Marrow and Ben Ladder. But I'd like to think that when you grow up, you grow out of your childhood entanglements. You go forward and you try not to look back and see what you left behind or missed out on. The boy died in me in Aberdeen, in Korea, and here in Marrow, when I learned about truth and why sometimes you don't want to know, though you have to keep trying to live. After the first child died, I wasn't sure Grace would endure the loss. She gazed at me as if I were empty, as if I didn't realize what had happened.

I know desire and love pass right on through some people, while in others they smolder or quietly die. They can be rekindled by a tender gesture, a sudden encounter, and a voice whispering a shared truth.

I know they can.

Apparitions

The invitations had been sent weeks before. Mercy and Ulla had been invited, and as a joke, Eunice dropped off one at the Sweet Hereafter Funeral Home, leaving the address blank, knowing Darleen would show it to Cane. Knowing, too, that Cane would never come. She'd heard a rumor that Cane had a beau and that made her spit with envy and disbelief. To help Nellie and Minish along in the world, Eunice had included them. She felt it was her job to be kind to them and allow them to experience some of the white pleasantries her Lyon name afforded.

Eunice had been granted the use of the cottage house on the Lyon estate for her Dumb Supper. Though she was King's cousin, she acted like she was queen of the place now that Miss Dunnet had died. She was determined to find a clue as to whom her beloved would be. And though she hadn't been too lucky at school meeting boys of distinction, she felt sure it was in her blood to marry a man with an honorable name and a good-paying job.

Though some of the womenfolk told her they had had their Dumb Suppers in May, Eunice had overheard her grandmother say the best time of the year was in September. September was the time of the year for growth, Eunice decided, her flat chest aside, so September it would be. Also, Mercy Haydon was still in town.

She heard the four girls approaching. She had instructed them to arrive exactly at the same time. They were requested to wear white dresses, fancy shoes, and bring a hostess gift.

"OK, y'all, this is how it works. We have to do everything backwards and eat our supper in silence, but before then, I can talk and open gifts on the porch. And when a suitor-spirit shows up we can all talk after he gives us a sign."

In the back of her mind, Eunice had to admit she was worried that no one or some evil sign would appear. One of her eyes had started to itch in anticipation of the event.

The cooling winds of September twirled around their necks as Eunice opened her gifts: watermelon syrup in a corked jug from Ulla, huckleberry and thimbleberry jam from Nellie and Minish, a book on Human Anatomy from Mercy.

"First we have to sweep the floor. And we all have to take turns."

The others nodded, willing to do whatever Eunice requested. This was an unusual event, but a coveted one, most of them aware they would never be invited to another supper with the same intention.

"Then we need to set the table with the china I borrowed from the big house. For good luck, we all get two forks."

"How do we know when someone has appeared before us?" Ulla asked. Her white dress sagged on her like flaps of skin.

"Ulla, you will know when you hear the sign. After we sit down, we must keep our eyes shut too." Eunice's mother had sent a dress from Durham that was blinding white and edged with red silk ribbon.

Nellie and Minish spoke to each other in finger code. They wore matching gingham dresses that made them look like dolls.

"If a white boy appears before me or Minish, do we have to take him?" Nellie asked.

Everyone paused to ponder the question.

"Don't you worry about that," Eunice said. "Even in the other world, they know the races don't mix. There's a colored boy for both of you."

"What do we do if nobody shows up?" Mercy asked, as she pulled a stray thread from her plain cotton dress. She had been thinking about this possibility since her invitation arrived. She wasn't much interested in boys and would be glad if no one came calling for her. She didn't really believe in superstitions anyway.

"I guarantee something will happen. Something always does, but if anyone speaks during supper before the suitor-spirit arrives, he will fade away and die. Die down dead." Eunice gazed out over the property and towards the sky as if she had the will to make the suitor show up and vanish.

"Dead," they all whispered, though Mercy figured as a spirit he was already half-dead, but she held her tongue.

Inside the cottage the girl-brides cleaned the dining room and set the table in silence. Each girl had an empty chair next to her. With five bodies moving about backwards, it was a feat to keep a straight face, much less keep from giggling and knocking into one another. When the work was completed, Eunice motioned to them all to sit down. She went to the front door and opened it, they all knew, so that the man of their dreams could glide right in. Eunice lit a candle and passed it around the table.

When the candle was in front of each girl, she gazed into the flame for a sign of things to come. The taper was supposed to have a golden wedding band around it, but Eunice could only find a fat candle and she had to use a napkin ring instead. When the candle was in front of Eunice the flame snapped like a firecracker. Nellie almost dropped the candle, her nerves getting the better of her. Minish smiled and combed back her hair as if her suitor could see her reflection. Mercy took a deep breath and tried to hold it until her turn was finished, but towards the end, she exhaled and the amber flame went out for a moment, and then re-lit itself. When the candle stopped in front of Ulla she tried to relax. A fall breeze curled the flame.

Ulla thought she saw an image in the center of the flame. Tears filled her eyes.

Eunice was about to hand Ulla a tissue when they all heard a thud. Nighttime had come, but nature had been as quiet as the supper, until now. The noise went around each side of the cottage without the girls seeing a soul. Eunice had warned them that often it took a future husband-spirit a while to show up and find his way in. They all spread their fingers out on the table and closed their eyes, as Eunice had instructed them to do. Up the five porch steps they heard the clump-thud-clump of their intended.

Mercy could hear the clock in the Lyon household ringing nine times. The clock in her own bedroom only worked if she laid it on its side. Ulla clinched her teeth and eyelids, trying to forget the image in the flame. Nellie swayed back and forth, bumping into Minish on occasion. Minish was convinced the noise had come knocking for her, so she made sure her back was straight and her ankles were crossed. Eunice had secretly gone to visit Granny Ma'am the year before about what to do at a Dumb Supper, to increase her chances of being successful. When it was clear somebody or something had passed through the doorway, she called out, "Whomever my true love may be, come and eat this supper with me." Eunice had been instructed by Granny Ma'am to snag the suitor-spirit first.

Eunice felt the heat of a body sitting next to her. She tried to smell him, to see if he were a spirit she recognized. He smelled like Scuppernong wine and this pleased Eunice, since it meant he was older. She heard the man slurp-up the supper she had left for him, and though she knew the other girls were bound to keep their eyes closed until the intended spoke, she knew they knew that the empty seat next to her had been chosen.

"I can't be your true love, Eunice, cause we're first cousins," said a voice they all recognized, even as it was spoken through a mouthful of Brunswick stew.

Ten eyes opened and laid their irritated glances on King. He smiled in a comfortable way and flashed the invitation in their faces. It had his name written neatly on the front.

King held his head high, but tried to look down to see how impressed the girls were with his arrival.

Minish and Nellie laughed. Mercy exhaled fully and blew out the candle in the middle of the table. Ulla's complexion had turned from white to gray-blue.

"King Lyon, this is a Dumb Supper, you get out of here right this minute!" Eunice said.

Eunice rolled her eyes so only the whites showed. It always scared King whenever she did it to him as a way of getting his candy or his allowance. He raced out of the house holding both pants pockets.

"Well, that ends it. Everyone here has a valid reason for not marrying King, so Ulla don't look so ill-to-your-stomach. Granny Ma'am gave me a backup plan in case this one failed. I guess she knew the spirit world better than we do. Say this over and over to yourself until your eyes close shop for the night,

> *"On Friday night I go to bed*
> *I put my petticoat under my head*
> *To dream of living and not the dead*
> *But dream of the man I'm going to wed."*

The other girls got up in unison, not saying a thing to their hostess, and marched though the door and down the steps sick of Eunice and mad as the devil.

Drawing with the Aid of the Sun

Jack Pliney and Cane met at the upper section of the Paw Creek. It was on land that no one had claimed, between the Lyon property and the Paradise Valley county line. No one owned it. Jack Pliney had checked, so he decided to quietly build a small cottage on the land and claim squatter's rights.

It was well before daybreak and that just suited Cane fine. The longer summer days made it harder for Cane to keep out of sight. She had carried some of her equipment up the pathways behind her house and over onto the ownerless acreage. She was giving Jack Pliney a photography lesson so he could photograph nature and how it was, for better or worse, changing. He'd decided to get one of those small cameras he'd seen in the paper. He wanted to be able to capture the underbellies of ferns, midget orchids, and the patterned motion of insects crawling around the red maples, laurels, and oaks. Cane's specialty was portraits, not doodads or nature, but she liked the idea of teaching Jack Pliney something.

"When photography first came about they called it drawing with the aid of the sun. I guess photography was as new to them as the television is to us. It helps to think about drawing when you set your shot. Think about what you want in your picture. Draw it with your eyes."

Cane adjusted the tripod so that it sank into the earth to hold it steady.

"That sounds dumb, I know, but it's true. Just like you would think ahead about planting a garden or fixing up a damaged one."

Cane finished attaching her Leica. She was trying to get Pliney to buy a used Leica, but Pliney wanted a new Kodak 35mm. This project he was working on was so important to him, he wanted the most modern equipment to make an accurate account of it. The beginners always thought new was better. Even Cane wanted the new Leica M3 she'd read about in her magazine, but she needed to save up for it and she knew most of the older cameras were better lasting anyway.

Pliney had told Cane that the land above town was pure and unafflicted until you reached the Lyon property. From then on as the Paw meandered into the Tear and the land flattened into the town square, the quality of the clay and water deteriorated. He wanted photographic proof of it.

"This is my tiny plot of heaven. When my body gives up the ghost, I want you to be sure that I'm buried here and nowhere else," Pliney said to Cane like she was kin. "Celie is already here. Down there nature is dog paddling in a sea of humans. Up here the odds are in favor of the flora and fauna."

"What does fauna mean?" Cane had to ask. She liked Pliney, but he often tossed big words right over her head. Also, she wanted to avoid the idea of his request. She didn't want to think about Jack Pliney as a dead man.

"The animals that live in our region; it comes from the Latin, meaning Roman goddess."

Roman goddess. "How?"

Pliney could be so sure about things when others were struggling for insight.

"Cane, it's just the root of the word. The origin, where the word came from. Like the Paw is the beginning here. The Paw is actually five crooked-looking creek fingers that meet at the palm or the start of the Tear. Roots are the beginning, but with time what comes from them can change or die out, just like Paw did, just like some languages do."

Cane put her camera in front of him so he could examine it. A Roman goddess, Cane said to herself.

"Everything has its own language and appears foreign at first." Pliney fumbled with the camera. "My mother collected and grew flowers and plants when I was young. She had her own flower-language that her folks had taught her."

Pliney looked around trying to locate something. "If I gave you a bouquet with Calla lilies, Yucca plant, Pansies, and Pysostegia my mother would see it as Jack-in-the-Pulpit, Tears-of-the-Lord, Johnny-Jump-Up, and Baptist Sister. That was her church bouquet. We all learn it a little different."

Pliney stopped and returned to the camera. "I see what I want, but the light? How do you set the light?"

Cane measured and rotated the ring on the camera to the correct setting. "Sometimes you just guess by your surroundings. After a while you look through the lens and know, you just know how much light you need. But up here you might need one of those flash bulb cameras that the newspaper men have."

Pliney shook his head, but proceeded to snap a few shots. "See there, see that wiggling orchid. We called her Bucking Bessie. She gets nervous at the least bit of noise, where other things out here shield themselves from light." He met Cane's eyes. "There's a wild black tulip that only raises its head at night. My ancestors on my mother's side called it Flower-that-Speaks-the-Language-of-the-Night. On my father's side his people called it the Queen of Africa."

Cane, too, studied flowers and knew what they meant. Ulla Trunk had returned a bunch of flowers from Winkie that had been "waylaid by accident" as Ulla put it to her. Cane could not understand why that girl put up with her father. The flowers were handed over all askew, but Cane understood their meaning. Reluctantly, it seemed to Cane, Ulla had handed over the arrowhead with the love note scribbled on it. Neither Ulla nor Cane could look each other in the eye in the dim light of her shop. Cane now wore the arrowhead on a silk cord hanging down her back.

"Taking pictures in the dark of night is a whole lot of trouble. I can't help you there," Cane said, though that wasn't really the truth. She'd done a study of night creatures at the Tear herself many years ago, but it wasn't the same as sitting by the edge of the water and watching. She loved her cameras but sometimes they left a blank spot where she needed a picture, a picture that could only come from her eyes seeing it right as it happened instead of through a lens. Especially at night when she loved to listen to the swish of the moccasins passing by or the hectic gatherings of the eaterbugs. The smell of the river coupled with the clay was enough, though after talking with Pliney, maybe there was danger in smelling the earth, or touching the water. She sat in the sand often and let her hands web out into the watercress and into the shallow sections of the Tear. One time when she was 15, before Pliney warned her to stay out of the Tear, she had waded into the middle and pulled out a soft looking branch. It was from a dogwood tree in bloom. The white flowers had stuck to the bark in a way that made the limb look alive, like a baby arm, or a snake. She'd painted her face with the wet red clay and pretended she was an Indian warrior.

Pliney shot the roll until the last frame cranked around. He kept clicking the camera until Cane touched his hand.

"You're done. You've used up 36 exposures. If you want, I can develop those for you. Or I can show you how to do that, too."

Pliney hesitated and Cane knew he didn't want to have to ask anything else of her. Daylight was shining through the canopy of trees. Cane would need to leave soon.

She took the camera off the tripod and set it back in her bag. Collapsing the metal tripod into a slender unit, she said,

"I was just joking with you. I'll develop it later and get it to you tonight or tomorrow night, Mr. Nature Scientist."

"I want to give you something for your trouble," Pliney said. "Last night I made these corn dumplings. My mother made them for me when I was younger. She said they helped babies thrive." He pulled out a bowl and uncovered it. Little balls were floating in liquid the color of the river.

Cane stepped forward and took the bowl.

"It's an Indian recipe. The mashed corn is mixed with wild Catawba grapes and then covered with sugarcane syrup. It's good for the baby, Cane."

Cane looked down at her belly and nodded. She tipped the bowl to her lips and let one dumpling fall into her mouth at a time. The syrup slathered her chin.

"What a mess I am," she said to Pliney. For the first time in a long while, Cane was content with herself. She departed before the morning light could lay its hands on her body.

Deficiencies in Anatomical Grace

Cane felt the last heat of Indian summer turning her body into an overcooked butterbean. If she could have lied down in wet clay she would have, but she was not sure if she'd be able to get back up, or if it was safe. The Cuffee Sisters had told her if she ever were with child, to stay away from swimming holes, mules, and red Carolina clay.

Darleen was on the porch, rocking back and forth, while Cane put a chair right up at the screen door to catch the breeze. Though her house wasn't on a main thoroughfare, she and her mother did get a good assortment of people walking by, taking the scenic way to town. Penny Steele huffed by and Cane thought she saw steam coming out of her pores.

"Afternoon, Miss Penny," Darleen said as she reached the edge of their property.

"After-damn-noon," Miss Penny said. "I declare this town is going to be the death of me, even before you planned to see me, Darleen. Did you know that the Methodist Home doesn't have room for Mama?" Miss Penny asked this more to the air than to Darleen. Miss Penny had a reputation for swearing whenever she opened her mouth. Her specialty was putting a cuss word right in the middle of another word. Her nine kids usually put their hands over their ears, or she did it for the one closest to her, if any were around.

"They say every-damn-body gets a fair shot, but I tell you they would find a space if it was one of the Lyon folk. It's not fair at all to Mama. It's not her fault we grew up poor and we look it. When poverty is your calling card, nobody in town

157

wants to be near you except others in the same predicament, or the church on the days they choose." Miss Penny nodded her head like a bird chewing seeds. "The charity folks are happy to step in and inspect your home at any time, too, as long as you are will-hell-ing to parade your private life in front of them so they can see you squirm and write down all the details in triplicate. And woe and damnation to you if your first child arrived before you had a chance to get married. They want to see all the birth, marriage, and death documents. Wouldn't surprise me if they had a contract with the govern-shit-ment to spy on us." Miss Penny paused and filled up her lungs.

"What are you going to do with your mama?" Darleen had to ask, and even Cane pressed her face into the screen to listen.

"My sister over in Wilson is going to come and fetch her for a while. What rich people don't understand is that we take care of our own kin, whether we can bear it or not. Poor people are everybody's keeper, when you think about it."

Darleen kept rocking in her chair, and the woman wiped her face and checked her clothing as if she were getting ready for another battle.

"Miss Penny," Cane called out, "why don't you see if she can get in at the Presbyterian Home, or the Baptist one on the outskirts of town?"

"Darleen, didn't you teach your child a thing about religion? Religion in our parts is like a crop. You don't mix it with others, Cane." Miss Penny collapsed her eyelids in an attempt to see Cane better.

"I hear them boys teasing you about your face, Cane. We all have deficiencies. We just keep on, just like you do. You just have to keep on and find your grace some-damn-where else."

With that Miss Penny forged ahead. They saw her bony body slip into the wilderness, like an offering that couldn't be ignored.

Cane moved away from the door to go pee. The peeing

never seemed to end. She went upstairs like she always did, so as not to get Darleen suspicious. The downstairs toilet had been put in special for Grandma Winnie, but nobody used it. If they ever had had company, it could have been the bathroom for guests, but as it was Darleen and Cane only had visitors on the porch. No one was invited any further.

At the top of the stairs Cane heard the drip-drip, pause, drip-drip into the tub. She'd remembered that noise since she was a baby. It was kind of like a lullaby to her. What she couldn't stand, though, was the rust stain that it left on the white porcelain. In the bathroom, there it was spreading like a diseased river. She reached for a cleaning cloth and put some cleanser on it. She bent towards the stain and tried with all her pregnant might to rub it clean. She'd tried in the past to remove the stain, but as her due date approached, she'd begun to scrub at it like an itch, like she'd been let out of the crazy house too early. Darleen told her everybody in town had a tub with a water trail. And was adamant that if anyone had a lily-white tub, it only meant they never took the time to clean themselves.

Pliney had told Cane it was the natural impurities that left their notice on her tub, but she knew Pliney also thought there was something dangerous that had seeped into the water underneath Marrow.

She went to her room and pulled out one of her cameras. She came back into the bathroom and finished a roll of pictures. Fifteen shots of the rust-colored water mark. Maybe Pliney could use this in his research someday, she thought.

Her room was now full of photography magazines, three cameras, a box full of lenses, the carousel-horse eyeball by her bed, dog-eared yearbooks from the high school, a dust-laden Singer sewing machine, the leftover bolt of plaid that her Grandma had left her, and an album of all the babies she had photographed. She had been willed four objects that had belonged to the Cuffee sisters. She was the proud owner of the three rocking chairs with the curious symbols. She'd put them out on the second-floor porch attached to her room. They had left her their circus trunk, too. Out of respect she had waited to open it until their death plots had settled and their markers were finished. Cane didn't want to pry into their business if their resting place wasn't complete.

It was a peeling steamer trunk with foreign spelling on it. With her small hands she was able to pry the lock open without damaging it. You could say her early experiences with taking things helped her to be gentle now. The sisters had specified that Cane was to get the trunk; most of the rest of their belongings were carted away to the dump. There was a rumor that after the chairs and the trunk were removed, the house was victim to an internal hurricane, the likes of which Sheriff Hayes had never witnessed. Even the man who lived at the dump said all the belongings arrived in pieces. There was nothing to scavenge, or someone or something had already done a powerful job of scavenging. The man at the dump said the belongings dispersed just at the moment they were being unloaded; swept away by an approaching tropical storm, wind patterns that had swirled up from South America.

The lock fell off into Cane's hands. She pushed open the top. There were a pair of seed-pearl slippers, the Cuffee sisters' circus costumes, and at the bottom, wrapped in a Mexican blanket, was a glass jar with three sections, where something had once been preserved. Cane pulled out the glass jar. At the bottom were chips of glittering stones. Emerald, ruby, and sapphire bits swam in a small gurgle of liquid.

"Whatever was here before?" Cane said to the trunk. The Cuffees had left no note or instructions. Cane took the jar to the bathroom and poured the jewels into her hand. She rinsed them off and they sparkled in a stream of rainbow light. Cane arranged them into a square and glued them onto a frame. She would put a picture of her family inside it.

Water Sounds
(Ulla)

Gossip is the language we speak in Marrow, and it is foreign to no one. Even the occasional visitor soon deciphers with ease the initially odd-sounding words and signals. Understanding French or the Bible is not as easy. Especially hearing the ones who preach for the Lord. Or even the Lord himself. Did you think, God, that I would endure forever? That the Reverend's words would heal me, that the marks would ever go away? Did you think that the death of my mother would somehow make me strong? Make me work harder to deflect the hunger from my father? They say that before this land became a worm's paradise, the well I stand in front of was used to give life; the water was used to bless children and deliver us from evil. Maybe that's its function. I had heard the pearly girls would throw their heavy bodies down this rocky tunnel to the cool waters below, in order to get some blessing before their end. The shame of an unknown father, the suitor that would not make his existence known, the obvious choice of sin was too great to bear in this town. Cut to the marrow. Ha! It would be better to suffocate in the womb of the water than to feel the pressure, the unyielding weight of his body above me. I ask you, I ask you why you would allow such possibilities in mankind? I asked you many times, but the only answer was the water calling to me. At first I thought it was the Tear River or Paw Creek. But there is too m͏ at either spot for regrets or escape. Here at the we͏ only one step to embrace.

I wonder who is already down there all these years. Mabel Smith has to be. Rumor has it the Conner sisters fell in together. Some serviceman from Paradise Valley got the better of them. Double trouble. Double death.

Are the protruding rocks marked by nail scratches? The outside of the well is so smooth. The inside is so unfinished. I wish I could fall down in slow motion and see the bits of the lives of the girls before me. A scrap of material, a faded picture, a broken mirror. I call down, 'Hello,' and someone answers back. Hello. Hello. Hello. I tried to obey. One night he wanted ham biscuits, red-eye gravy, and Aunt Suki's squash casserole right away. He said, "I'm so hungry, Ulla, my belly thinks my throat's cut." I tried to be quick about it. The ham wasn't burnt enough. I had forgotten how he enjoyed peeling-off blackened skin. Since you left me, Mama, Father only broke his promise three times. Fathers come first, is how he explained it, laughed it away. I could stand the ones in town who knew and looked the other way. I heard the whispers and the giggles. The heads that shook didn't bother me. It was those children. The two little ones who came to me yesterday and asked in a jumble of childish sounds with words someone had put in their mouths. "Is it true your daddy . . ." Their tiny hands were pudgy and smeared with dirt. Their faces were glazed with sun. The smocking on their dresses was dainty, a line of ducklings, and a spray of dogwood. ". . . stuck his peanut in your shell?"

I am not sorry for anyone. And I hope no one is sorry for me. Silence became my next-of-kin. Silence made herself my only friend. Silence, Silence, never give up on her.

I won't be needing the suit the Cuffee sisters' sent. I've wrapped it up with Mercy Haydon's name on it, propped it against the shiny speckled rocks that line the outside of the well. I remember that folks would rub them for good luck. I did, too, when I was young.

I can't see if any light shines on the surface of the well water. It is dark around His Glory and looking downward, too. The water slaps the side of the rock tunnel. How can there be waves inside this well? I hear them again.

Mama, will you be there to catch me?

Tending the Dead

Somehow sitting on a blanket in the dirt, letting the earth carry the weight of her body, calmed Cane. She had a ritual of going to His Glory once a month just to visit the graves of the dead babies she'd photographed. It was harder tonight, now that she was pregnant, without the light of the moon to guide her around the grave markers and wedges of dirt and other objects that heaved above ground at times. But she'd come to His Glory since she was born and she knew it by heart, stone for stone. She'd carry tiny bouquets that wouldn't last long or cause much notice. The relatives of the deceased children often came to see the graves for a few months after the service. If she placed a small bunch of flowers at the site, no one would suspect it was her doing. Through the years she'd discovered that people were coming to His Glory to visit the departed less and less. More dead were moving in, but the ritual of grieving and of clearing and honoring the gravesite was less popular than she remembered. There was a time when she was young, when she'd seen whole families visiting on Sundays with picnic baskets and tools to keep up the family marker. The gesture honored the living as well as the deceased. Now some of these graves were lucky if their kin came once a year. People seemed to have their minds on other things, or they just forgot, or worst of all they didn't care to remember. Even though Cane hadn't liked her Grandma Winnie, she still tended her grave.

The groundskeeper at His Glory worked to the bone during the light hours, but mostly he just tried to keep nature from overtaking the cemetery. All the churches in town had their own sections, and with the town mayor they helped pay the groundskeeper's salary. Though it was his duty to care for the graves, he didn't have enough time to get to all of them. The Lyon family had Jack Pliney care for their mausoleum and surrounding land, but most folks left it to the groundskeeper who had been doing the same job the same way since anyone could remember.

For the babies she'd photographed, on each tiny grave Cane placed a handful of blossoms tied up with white ribbon. Some folks had small marble crosses or simple markers. Those with more money had angel statues or lambs sleeping peacefully looking over the deceased. Miss Dunnet's babies had cradle-shaped markers with a likeness of the child carved out of the stone, stone blankets covering it, and a marble-veined mother's hand reaching over to comfort the child.

With all the babies, Cane mouthed their lullabies as if she were the mother. If she were sure no one was around, she'd sing out loud. Cane believed that the tone of the lullaby, the soft sweet sound of a mother's voice, helped the child sleep. The words to some of the lullabies she knew seemed tragic, dangerous, or even sinister. Cane sang "Joe Monroe" to all of the dead Dunnet babies. If any of those babies had lived and learned the words to their song of comfort, they would have died of fright. But maybe the song kept the evil away like a warning, maybe tradition dictated passing down the good and the not-so-good.

Sitting on a blanket near the Dunnet plot, Cane felt a wisp of air tickle her spine. The wind's fingers wrapped around her shoulders, squeezed and moved on, a sign from Madame Nature that the seasons were about to shift. Cane's busiest time of the year, winter, would be arriving soon, as it always did. Even if it was a mild winter, the graveyard would be full. Grandma Winnie had told her God and the Devil had nothing to do with nature and her cycles. It was just Madame Nature doing her business on her own.

"Just ponder it," she would say, "I'm a God-fearing woman, but more than once Madame Nature put the fear of death in me with her hurricanes cavorting up and down the coast, her dancing tornadoes in the mid-states, and the earthshakers out West." She would go on to explain, "You could just expire from nature, natural causes, and not have a leaning about God, one way or the other."

Yes. Yes, Cane remembered, "The Wind Lullaby."

> *Go to sleep, go to sleep*
> *Go to sleep, little baby*
> *Mama run away, Papa wouldn't stay*
> *Left nobody but the breeze and baby.*

That would do for Riley Trunk because it was about someone who was left with nothing.

Cane had asked Darleen once about the lyrics of the songs she had sung to Cane.

"Mama wasn't well and her maids sang me to sleep," Darleen had told her. "They had been sung to by their mamas and their mamas before them. They tell a story and sometimes stories aren't so sweet. But words don't matter so much. I could have said anything to you, if I used my kind voice. It always did the trick with you."

Cane hated to think her mother was right, though she knew words did matter later on. Lullabies carried messages of a family past. They were secret codes of love and struggle. They were often the first sounds and words a child heard, and they could mark a future. Cane kept coming to the cemetery to keep the babies' history alive. When she was gone though, she didn't know anyone who would carry on that tradition. After seeing so many people come through her shop, mostly dead, but some young and some well on their way in life, she knew that some traditions and rituals had to end, and some just did without a fight or even much notice. But as long as she was able, these babies would be sung to, even if she had to carry her own child with her to His Glory.

Potions From Florida

ane hadn't seen Winkie Jr. for a spell. The last thing he'd left her was a bird feather wreath nailed to the wall of her shop. It had chirp berries and lace-shaped fronds attached to it. Jack Pliney thought it looked like a garland the Paw Creek Indians offered to their friends from other tribes. Cane thought it looked like a nest, at least she hoped that's what Winkie Jr. had been striving for. When Darleen saw it, she wanted it for her latest customer since it would last longer than most funerary wreaths and she could charge extra. But Cane told her mother that she had made it for Ulla Trunk, to hang at the well. And though Darleen didn't care a dime about Riley, she did feel badly about how things worked out for Ulla, so she let it go.

Even Winkie Jr.'s father had called Darleen's shop to see if anyone had seen hide or hair of him. Cane wasn't worried, she just missed him, more than she'd expected. She marked it off as femaleness. Everything she did seemed harder to do and exaggerated. Orders were down a bit and she was relieved. The smell of the developing chemicals, once sweet to her, were now enough to clear out her gut.

Instead of working she put her head down on her desk each afternoon and dreamed about the baby. A few of the visions woke her up in a creek of sweat. She dreamed about names, ones that never made sense like Pinenut or Cornpone and ones that did, Buckford, Winnefred, and Jack.

It felt like summer weather though it was late autumn. Part of the Beaver Moon could be seen all day, and at sunset it was supposed to be the largest moon of the year. A full moon, like the one Cane was carrying around. My sweet-as-Winkie child.

Just as Cane prepared to go, she peered out from behind her curtains and saw the red glow of the day ending and the white heat of the night light spreading. There were lizards on her window screens; they had stayed late this year. One of them clawed at the humidity like it was the enemy, jumped towards it, leaving its tail dangling in the metal mesh. It was a comfort that a lizard could just grow another tail if some incident in nature or man caused the tail to separate from its body.

The front door opened just as Darleen came through the side door. The look on Winkie Jr.'s face as he stepped in, first full of syrupy love and desire that could walk by itself, careened into seriousness at the sight of Darleen.

"Miss Walker," he said looking between the women. Winkie was carrying a basket full of items covered with a cloth that had the state of Florida outlined on it.

"Your daddy is sure looking for you, young man," Darleen said eyeing the basket and unaware that Cane hadn't yet taken her eyes off Winkie. "Just the other day he called here asking about you."

"Miss Walker," Winkie replied still talking to the imaginary line separating the females, "I took a holiday to visit some relatives in Florida."

Cane couldn't help the "Huh" that came out of her mouth. But Darleen snickered with such vigor that she muffled out Cane's response.

"Don't you try to fool me, Winkie Jr. I bet you're in a heap of trouble. As my mama told me, a lie will run itself to death. Believe you me, I know."

Winkie smiled straight across his face.

"Mama, I remember Winkie Jr. mentioned a while back that his mama's folks were from down that way."

Darleen looked over to Cane and made an "umph" noise, like she couldn't quite decide who was lying.

"I just came by to see if your daughter had time to take a portrait picture of me, to send to my kin as a remembrance." Winkie pulled out a pomegranate from the basket and gave it to Darleen. "Here. This is one of the crazy fruits they have down there. It looks kind of leathery on the outside, but inside it's red, with sweet, juice-filled beads. It's the food of the underworld, or so they say."

The offering appeased Darleen long enough to remind her it was time to leave work. She had failed to notice that Cane kept her face unshielded in the light of the doorway and that Winkie looked straight at her now, instead of looking away.

"Well, suit yourself with Cane. She's been a lazy sow for weeks. If I didn't know better, I'd think she had some of that slow blood you see in the coloreds and Indians around here." With that, Darleen went back over to her shop.

Cane and Winkie focused on that side door until they heard Darleen's front door open and close. They waited until they heard her walk down the street, her flat pumps slapping the sidewalk like an insult. Even then, they waited an extra minute, before they started moving their limbs toward each other. "I brought you these funny gifts from Florida."

Winkie put the basket on the table. He grabbed for her ring finger to hook it like they always did. "Look, they're called alligator pears," he said, bringing out the bumpy-skinned avocados. "And these are wild swamp-plums and horse-bananas. They have odd-looking and -tasting eats down there."

Winkie gazed at Cane. She opened her work coat and he dropped his eyes to her belly. His mouth fell open and not a word came out.

Cane pulled his hand to her. "It's OK, Winkie, it's just the baby growing." She put her hand on his belly. "Looks like I'm not the only one eating up a storm."

Winkie laughed. "I stopped at the side of the road on my way back, at the Florida border, and an old man and woman were selling produce. I told the woman my sister was going to have a baby, and I asked her what was best for the mother. She gave me all this stuff." Winkie lifted a mango from the bottom of the basket. "She said this would help you the most, though the other fruit is good, too." The mango was the size of a prize-winning sweet potato; it had yellow-green skin with black spots all over it.

Cane whiffed at the sugary smell that lingered in front of her nose.

"Did you really visit your kin in Florida?"

"Yeah, my father calls Florida the step-sister of the South. He says it should have broken off and attached itself to Cuba. I don't think he likes my mama's folks. They treated me good, though." He took out his pocketknife and peeled back the skin of the mango. "I had to go find my way."

Cane came forward and Winkie slipped a piece of the flesh between her lips. He had to grasp the fruit and Cane sucked on his fingers in order to keep the fruit from falling between them.

"I stuffed myself with gator steaks, cooter, and rattlesnake. That's why I'm so full looking." He draped his hand over his protruding belly and then moved his hand to hers, like a fern shading a wild orchid. "And I swallowed the snake meat, too. I didn't spit it out like most folks."

"Come," Cane said. "No one the right size has rolled in to claim the giant catafalque, but with all our eating, I hope we still fit." She'd be sure to ask Pliney about the eating of snakes, if it was helpful or hurtful.

Cane and Winkie Jr. lay together like river otters snuggling in moist clay. Winkie tried to sleep, but the movement of the baby kept opening his eyes. The truth will keep your eyes open, he thought. Cane shivered with him next to her again.

The ancient kind of shiver that makes bones shift. She breathed fully as she raised her baked-potato-looking feet.

"I'm scared for you, Cane." Winkie said. He knew she hadn't told her mother and he was glad. Unlike most people in town he wasn't scared of Darleen, but he hadn't figured out how the public knowledge of Cane being pregnant by him would sit with her or anybody else. He hadn't told a soul. From his pocket he pulled out a tan shark's tooth the size of a small fist. It had tiny points all around the sides. "It's a fossil. A long time ago, there were river sharks in Florida. And this is what's left of them. The old woman told me to take this to the father for good luck."

Cane put her hand around the tooth. "I wonder if they ever lived in the Tear?" Sharks would account for a few of the unexplained incidents in the river, though not for the ones she — and she suspected Jack Pliney — had caused. She touched the end too hard and punctured her finger. She put her finger up to her mouth, but Winkie caught it instead. The blood filled out into a bubble. "I'm fine, Winkie."

Winkie took the fossil tip and poked his own finger.

"Let's have a blood marriage right here, OK? We put our fingers together and promise to be with each other till death sniffs us out."

As they sat up and stepped out of the catafalque, the first drop of blood got away from Cane, but Winkie caught it in the tiny pool of blood on his finger.

"Till death sniffs us out."

Mark of Mercy
(Mercy)

Mother dragged Lily and me to church. It was a first for both of us as far as we could remember. Usually, we found the Lord some other way, playing Bible hangman or sketch-a-scripture. I had heard the soup-to-nuts in my 15 recordings. But this particular Sunday, Reverend Mitchell was away and the replacement was a young man just out of Yale Divinity School. Visitors from fancy schools carried a lot of weight with folks around here. Mother was hell-bent and determined to go; I guess for a new view on an old story. We almost talked Daddy into going with us this one time, except his mother rang up saying the Lord was waiting for him with her. Anyway, my mother's sweetheart, Mr. Ladder, was going to go, too, after a long absence from church. I could see him getting ready to go and knew that his wife, Miss Ina, was all aflutter. Usually, she walked those two blocks down and three blocks over by herself to the Presbyterian Church. Today there would be a herd of worshippers. And she would be proud to shepherd us along.

When people in Marrow went to church, they usually had to just walk out a door and down the way or around the corner, depending on their faith. The Catholics had a tougher time. There were only eight members in town and they had a small church on the backside of the cemetery. It was also a caretaker's cottage and storage house for the remains from the circus that hadn't sunk into the earth, like the fortune wheel and a metal cage that the members walked through to get to their seats. They were the most accommodating faith. If I could have chosen, I would have been Catholic; you could always buy or pray yourself out of trouble. Anyone who wanted to worship with them was welcome with open arms. You couldn't say the same for Reverend Mitchell's church. Guess that's why today the sanctuary was full up. Of course, it was the second Advent Sunday, too.

We met the Ladders on our way. Mama was in her lime-green suit with the bone buttons. She was the only person I knew who could wear lime green in winter and still look right. She was wearing her green-and-cream leather pumps. Lily and I wore similar-looking dresses. I hadn't expected to be home from nursing school so soon, so I just pulled out my Christmas dress from last year and removed the beaded holly pin. Lily had made a new dress for this year out of the leftover material. We looked like fat bluebirds.

It took about three minutes to get to church. On the way, Lily managed to cozy up to Mrs. Ladder. She wanted rabbit-breeding advice. When we walked into church and down to the pews, Lily, Mother, and Miss Ina went first. The row they chose was about filled, so I had to sit behind them with Mr. Ladder. Just my luck. The program was hand printed and had a holiday wreath on the front; they wanted to impress the Northerner. I flipped through it, glad to see the hymns I could sing. If it hadn't been almost Christmas, I wouldn't have known any. Lily turned her head my way and looked at me like I was a Martian.

"Mercy, the visiting minister is speaking about you!" she said. She never knew when to shush. I ignored her, but slowly turned the stiff pages to the sermon section. Today's sermon, it read, was entitled, "The Mark of Mercy." I felt my face turn pale. I was sure he would be speaking something revealing about me and my family. As the congregation filled up the pews, no one else looked my way. I did notice Cane Walker half-sitting in the last pew of the church, ready to bolt if she had to. No one ever saw her during this time of day. She was wearing a black hat with a lace veil. Around her body she wore a huge coat. It looked like a man's coat, big enough for two people. Why she was here, nobody knew. Though Mr. Ladder nodded to her, and when Betsey Sunn came in dressed like the Queen of Sheba, she patted Cane's hand as if she were her child.

Reverend Mitchell's assistant started off the service with announcements about upcoming church events, and the member health watch, or death watch, as some called it. He was known for telling more particulars about church members than people ever wanted to hear. Eunice said every time they named an ill person in need of prayer, it seemed like they died the next week.

"The annual Christmas Bazaar will take place as usual on Christmas Eve. We are thankful that Mrs. Ina Ladder will head the event as she has done for the past 18 years."

Many from the congregation turned and smiled at Mrs. Ladder. I noticed that Mr. Ladder tried hard but couldn't help himself as he gazed at my mother's neck and the strands of hair curling at her collar. I noticed that with his gaze he commanded my mother to turn around, and she fought the urge, I could tell, but gave in halfway and looked at me.

"We are saddened to announce," the assistant continued, "that just this morning we heard about the passing of Riley Trunk." A curt silence took over the room. A few burning candles near the altar popped. I swear I heard Cane Walker gasp. "His body apparently found its way into the Tear River. With the recent winter rains, it worked itself all the way to Wilmington where it washed out into the Atlantic and then washed back up on the banks of Wrightsville Beach. As you can imagine, his body was much decomposed. A passerby found his Social Security card and a photograph in his wallet that indicated he was from Marrow, but before the authorities could rescue him, another storm washed his body out to sea again. It has yet to be found."

Miss Ina turned towards us, "There was no one here in Marrow to claim him anyway and no plots were ever purchased. I guess my poor Rachel had a vision about how things would turn out." Her voice was glasslike, not harsh or hurtful, but fragile in a way that made me sad for her for the first time in my life.

"We hold the Trunk family in our thoughts and ask that you all say a silent prayer for the passing of Riley Trunk."

I heard Lily whisper her prayer, *Stinker, Stinker, pumpkin eater, had a wife and couldn't keep her, put his child inside his shell, there he kept her till she fell.* I could see over my mother's shoulder that she traced her finger up and down her jacket. Most people's prayers were short. I didn't have anything to add. I only knew that Ulla had killed herself, and that didn't make sense because killing yourself was a sin, but I still missed her. And according to Eunice it had a lot to do with her father not being a father at all.

"Today's scripture reading will be offered by Betsey Sunn. She'll be reading from Romans 5:18-20. We are honored that Dr. Hubert Knox, from Yale Divinity School will be giving the sermon today. We thank him for taking this journey south, into our small town of Marrow."

I'd never heard of a woman reading scripture before. I knew now why Miss Sunn was in her regal outfit. She rose from her seat and stepped onto the pulpit. She spoke from memory.

"Then as one man's offense led to condemnation for all men, so one man's act of righteousness leads to acquittal and life for all man. For as by one man's disobedience many were made sinners, so as by one man's obedience many will be made righteous. Moreover the law entered, that the offense might abound; but where sin abounded, grace did much more abound."

Mercifully, her reading was brief. I had studied religion in school, but we never made it out of the Old Testament. I didn't know Romans from Corinthians. A well of confusion was filling up in my stomach though and giving me a bellyache. We sang, "O Come, O Come Emmanuel," and on this Sunday, at this church only, the women were supposed to sing, at Dr. Knox's request. I guess so the menfolk and boys could admire our sweet-sounding vocal cords. Though I was looking straight ahead at the Sunday School kids dressed up as angels near the altar, I could pick out each female voice around me. Lily had a tiny, almost baby voice. She should have been up there with the angels. Mama and Betsey Sunn had strong voices that mixed together. Miss Ina had a soft voice that carried the tune but not much else. Mitty Hyde and her group of ladies thought they could sing, but they all were off-key and didn't know it. Eunice couldn't remember the words — she was too busy looking around for boys — so she just hummed bits of the tune when she felt she needed to. I had been practicing the Christmas hymns at school and I thought I sounded pretty well. But I recognized Cane Walker's voice like the white-throated sparrow I'd heard when I was younger. Daddy would sit me on his knee on the porch and we'd listen to it sing the morning into being.

I didn't want to turn to look at her, but I had to see if it was true, if she was really attached to the sparkling sound coming form the back of the church. As I turned a bunch of other people did, too. For once, Cane had a bevy of folk looking at her, but not at her face. Such attention disturbed her, I could tell. She couldn't help but put her hands to her face as the hymn ended, muffling her contribution.

Dr. Knox was lean and not elderly, unlike Reverend Mitchell. He had red hair that had turned blonde at the ends. At least I only had a few bits of red. He stepped forward like he had known us our entire lives. He took a moment and observed us in silence. Lily picked up the donation pencil and started drawing on the envelope that came with it.

"I thank you for welcoming me to your house of worship. It is an honor to be here today on the second Advent Sunday. I heard the news of Mr. Riley Trunk's passing. A man I did not know." He paused and looked straight at me. I didn't know Mr. Trunk either. Ulla kept clear of him and said little about her home life, especially after her mom died. "Who here really knew him? Who really knows any of us? Outward appearances they say are misleading. Is it not the spirit of a person we embrace?" Lily's pencil broke in half and my mother opened her purse and handed Lily a pen.

Lily turned around to me with her lips pouted in disappointment. "I guess it's not about you, but about Mr. Trunk." Mother turned to both of us and pinched her tongue and twisted the tip of it. Her sign for us to zip it up or face the consequences.

"I ask all of you here in the congregation: Who in this town deserves forgiveness, who in this town have you misjudged, who has sinned and repented, but you hold only their sins in your thoughts and worse in your hearts? I ask you." He paused and put his hands together making a prayer house. "We are all marked with His mercy. Sometimes it is a physical sign, sometimes the mark is not so clear, but we are all marked. God can be subtle. His ways of working can blossom inside of us without our immediate knowledge."

"I urge you all on this second Sunday of Advent in the name of the Father, the Son, and the Holy Ghost, to embrace the mark of mercy God has bestowed on you, and, further, to find in the heart of your mind the gift of forgiveness in others who have sinned, and in yourself. Once we are forgiven, God does not want us to linger on the sin. There is a habit of living, a pattern you abide by when you accept the path

God has shown you. Reach out to your neighbor, reach into your soul, and be merciful and forgiving. Grace rises above sin, as we learned from the scripture reading. Reconcile yourself to grace, the grace of God. Come alive with the spirit God has given you. Jesus Christ was born in Bethlehem and God marked him, too. God marked him, too — for us."

By now, Dr. Knox was well into a full sweat. Lily stole a look at me and mouthed. "It's about Mom." From my seat, I could tell the minister needed some Spicy Talc. I was scared for myself because I couldn't figure out exactly what he was saying to me, and what it meant for my life, my future. Was I supposed to forgive Ulla? And where was my mark? Lily pulled up her hem and tried to find a sign on her knees. Most of the congregation just sat deaf and dumb like turnips until he finished.

"There is one thing I am sure of, as a friend of mine, Minister Fosdick, reminded us in one of his great sermons: Courtesy and kindness and tolerance and humility and fairness are right. Opinions may be mistaken; love never is."

Mrs. Ladder turned my way. I was the fork in the road today, but the look on her face was one of concentrated thought, like a recipe she'd forgotten had come to her almost, or a certain smell had wafted by her and she recognized the scent but couldn't name it. Since she put all her faith in the Church it never occurred to her to question the love of her husband. We were more alike than I ever imagined. She wanted what could never be.

Two ushers passed around the collection plate, and Mama put a few dollars in Lily's illustrated envelope. We sang one more hymn, "Lo, How a Rose!" before the choir and the Sunday School angels marched out. Then Dr. Knox slowly walked up the aisle with his arms wide to the side, his palms open like he was a gathering flowers or weeds. I noted that Cane Walker had already departed. How I wanted to closely examine her face for clues. And what had she done to be in such need of forgiveness? She must have done something. What had I done? We formed a line to thank the visiting minister like you always had to, even if he left you muddled to the core. We were near the end of it since we all had taken so long to collect each other. Lily dawdled as usual, snapping up extra programs while Mrs. Ladder was speaking to a neighbor about her holiday bazaar. With Mr. Ladder directing all of us we walked ahead of him. Lily was first, then me, then Mama, then Mrs. Ladder, then Mr. Ladder. I was glad for that order to be in place.

"Where is your mark?" Lily asked Dr. Knox as she reached for his hand. "Who have you forgiven?" He smiled and looked toward the cross above the altar. "My mark of mercy, I think, is that God allows me to preach to people, and sometimes the people listen, and sometimes they carry my message onward and sometimes they are just happy when the noon bells ring." He held Lily's hand and placed his other hand over hers. "Today I forgave Riley Trunk. I did not know the man, but I could tell he was in need of our prayers and forgiveness, even if we didn't like him or his ways. And that he won't have a Christian burial is especially sad."

Lily puckered her face and drew back her hand. "Well," Lily said, loud enough for most of the leftover congregation to hear. "I guess you won't be staying long in town, but I forgive you." She skipped down the steps.

I followed behind her, nodding at the visitor, well aware that the walk home would seem longer and be uncharacteristically quiet.

The Sacred Compunction
(1920s-1930s)

*P*eople *said they were more like brother and sister rather than childhood friends. But all Ben and Grace knew at first was that they were neighbors. Why they protected each other from the get-go and knew each other's world like twins do, neither understood.*

The time Grace tried to save Ben was when they were selling magazine subscriptions door to door. Ben hadn't learned to read as well as Grace. Grace fell out of her mother's womb with a book in her hand and was speaking more than necessary by the time she was two, or that's what her mother always told her and Ben. Children should be seen and not heard was a phrase foreign to Grace Palmer. Ben marched right up to the Rayford's porch. The Rayford family had a long line of large families. Families so big, people just shook their head in wonderment of the lot of them. "God will provide," Mama Rayford was heard to say daily until she didn't wake up one morning, and Mama's daughter Jellie had to step up to the plate as the new Mama Rayford.

"Ben, hold up. Can't you read the signs?" Grace reached for Ben, but he was already ahead of her with his skipping feet. The Public Health Department had given out quarantine signs for families who were ill or diseased. Most folks in Marrow had one sign up every now and then, but the Rayfords kept three signs attached to their front window—Scarlet fever, Mumps, Measles — as often as not.

Ben turned to her and then turned towards the window. He slowly read out the letters and sounded out the diseases like they were school spelling words or words from the Bible.

"They leave those up so salesmen won't knock at their door." He stepped forward and rang the bell. Grace kept her distance. She'd read

about consumption, plagues, foul-smelling illnesses and wanted nothing to do with them or that house. She was sure the diseases remained like earth-trapped ghosts with the rest of the Rayford brood. Their schoolmate, Duke Rayford, opened the door.

"Is your mama at home, Duke?" Ben asked. "We have important business with her."

Duke looked beyond Ben and waved to Grace. He puckered his lips and sent a stream of kisses her way. Grace put up her arms as if to fight them off.

"We don't want your silly magazines. Can't you see the placards in the window? We are sick in this house. Deadly ill." Duke took in a breath and blew it out all over Ben before he could step away. "Now you better not kiss your girlfriend or she'll die." Duke shut the door slowly so Ben could hear him laughing behind it and the laughter continued as if Duke knew that Ben would stand there until it faded out.

"Come on, Ben," Grace said. "We don't need the Rayfords. Mama thought the Lyons would buy some for sure." She stepped up to the porch just long enough to tug at his shirt. She walked ahead of him towards the Lyon property. Along the way she made him stop at Paw Creek and wash his hands and face.

"Do you think it's true?" Ben asked. He ended up washing his face, arms, and feet, just in case he tracked some of the diseases through his shoes. He dried off on the guinea grass.

"Duke's not sick. I know for a fact. He was at school all week," Grace said. "I just don't like germs." But she wondered if the infected air would harm her friend. Ben made motions to the side that Grace couldn't see, as if there was someone else in the conversation.

"I mean, if I kiss you, will you die?"

Grace looked at Ben. Her parents kissed her on occasion. Her grandparents made her kiss them when they visited.

"Kiss my pinkie finger. If I survive that, then you can kiss me on the face."

Ben took her little finger and kissed it quickly. Five minutes passed. They looked at each other, waiting for a sign. A whippoorwill cried out. The creek water seemed to rise up on the bank, but Grace kept on living. She gave Ben a nod and he approached her. He gently kissed her face.

Nothing happened, except they agreed they wouldn't tell a soul.

The time Ben tried to save Grace was years later when she was getting ready for her senior prom. Ben was walking with her to the dance, but he was not her date. She made a point of telling her girlfriends that Benjamin Ladder was like a cousin to her, even her parents thought of him as their kin. She'd turned down other boys who had asked her. Grace had wanted to arrive with someone, but be free to dance with whomever she liked.

That evening her parents had gone to a party at the Lyon household, confident that Benjamin Ladder would be by shortly to pick up Grace and assured that he was not a boyfriend, so the usual concern about the opposite sex did not apply.

Grace let him inside her home. She still needed to put on her silk shawl that matched her dress. It was slender, the kind that dangled over her arms, without any other function. Her elbow length gloves had come from Atlanta, a gift from her mother. They were outlined with beads that shimmered above each elbow with a transparent glow.

Ben choked at the sight of her.

"Grave Calmer, Grave Calmer," he said using his nickname for her, trying to hide his percolating desire. He'd been using that nickname since they started meeting at the Lyon Mausoleum every Christmas Eve. As Ben and Grace would walk past the graves, Grace would talk to them as if they were live people. "Now Mr. Sunn, I want you to know that Betsey is keeping herself busy." Or, "Aren't you glad, Mrs. Spikes, that Mr. Spikes followed you so soon?"

Grace looked back at Ben and saw the beginnings of a man. Grace turned back to the hall mirror. When she looked at herself, she saw Ben looking at her, looking like the Ben she'd always known. She reached towards the mirror to wipe off a smudge, a dash of something that was in the way of her full view. She tried too hard to remove it. The family mirror, an heirloom handed down on her mother's side, *veered to the right and then to the left, before it fell forward, almost knocking Grace on the head. Ben grabbed for Grace while the mirror fell to the floor and shattered into so many pieces that for years to come members of the family would get jabbed with the shards.*

"If you had let it fall on me, it wouldn't have broken," Grace scowled.

They looked down at the numerous reflections of themselves. Bits and pieces spread out over the wooden floor.

"I couldn't save you and the mirror," Ben replied, still holding onto Grace's arm.

"You can't fix a mirror," said Grace in a voice she used just for Ben. She looked into his face. "It would have done me good to get knocked in the head. Now, it's seven years bad luck for me."

She'd remembered Granny Ma'am's warning to her and her friends that a broken mirror meant lovers had quarreled. She put her hand up and stopped just before touching Ben's cheek, "And maybe seven for you, too."

Ben couldn't let go of her arm. He wanted to tell her all the feelings he had hovering inside of him. They had always been closer than blood like the limbs of a magnolia tree he'd seen that grew down, not up, limbs that met and re-rooted together underneath the earth's surface. Instead, he went to get the broom. If they were quick about it, they would still make it to the prom. They had to show up at the school dance or else people would really be talking. But first they had to find someone to replace the mirror.

Grace and Ben walked, aching and squeaking in their new attire, across the road and rang the bell at Betsey Sunn's home. She'd probably heard the racket anyway, and they decided confessing the problem to her was better than hiding it from her. Grace knew, too, from her mother that if you let Betsey Sunn into your secret world, she liked being a part of something others didn't know about.

As it turned out, Betsey Sunn was related to the glass man in the next town over. He took his sweet time, but came by and replaced the mirror glass. He kept referring to Grace and Ben as "the love birds."

"They have known each other most of their life. They're like siblings. Brother and sister. It almost wouldn't be right for them to be boyfriend and girlfriend," Betsey Sunn had said.

Grace was sure Miss Sunn must be thinking of her own husband, Chester. Betsey Sunn's true love had died in a train wreck in South America. "Especially, since they broke the mirror."

The glass man nodded. Grace and Ben studied their shoes. Everyone knew broken mirrors had a devil's list of bad omens attached to each craggy piece. Ben noticed how a shard stuck in his shoe and, if he looked closely, he could see one of his eyes but not both. He let it stay so he could show it to his buddies at the prom. The man set the mirror in the frame and hooked it back onto the wall. He added an extra nail to secure the frame. "Only God could bring down this mirror now."

Grace and Ben took the short cut by Paw Creek and through the cemetery to the high school. They walked as quiet as the graves. Jack Pliney, the Lyon's new gardener, was tending the Lyon plot. They barely saw him; his color gave him the gift of disguise. Next Christmas Eve, they would have to sneak around him, but on this day they nodded and smiled themselves into innocence.

They arrived just in time for the crowning of King and Queen of the school. Grace's girlfriends bugged their eyes and tapped their watches when Grace walked over to them.

"Grace Pearl," her friend Rose said, "You missed it when they announced you as Most Talkative." Rose pulled at Grace's gloves. "If the shoe fits! Your side-kick was named Quietest," she whispered. Rose faced Ben. "Evening, Ben." Ben nodded back, still savoring the implications of their late arrival. "I was hoping, Ben, you would win the Sealtest Ice Cream Eating contest this year so we could all ride in that red Oldsmobile. That was first prize. Too bad. Duke Rayford made a pig of himself." Rose held onto the edge of Ben's cuff. "Save a dance for me," she said. Ben gazed at her and then over to Grace who was busy chatting with her other friends. "I'm no good at it, Rose," he said taking a step backwards. "I'm real clumsy, just ask Grace."

STEPHANIE McCOY / 188

Ben wandered over to the boy's side of the auditorium. He maneu-vered around dancing couples and dangling decorations.

"You are awfully late, son," his friend Mitch Butler said. "It's about time you got somewhere with Her Graciousness." Color drained from the rest of Ben's body and pooled at his cheeks. His one other friend, Arthur Bingham, who had been named Most Intellectual, socked Ben in the arm. "You tarried at the gate, again?"

"The mirror at Grace's house fell off the wall and crashed into smithereens," said Ben trying to manage, without success, the mani-festations of his emotions. He showed them the shard still protruding from his shoe. "Once we kissed twice, though."

His two friends stared as if they never expected Benjamin Ladder to have achieved such a goal. They closed in on him as if he suddenly was a new boy instead of the one they had grown up with. Within hearing range, but not in their view, Grace filled up her cup with sas-safras punch. She had yet to be asked to dance.

"Swear on the Bible," Arthur said, pulling out a miniature one he carried with him.

Ben placed both hands on the black leather book. He stepped back looking bigger than he was.

"I swear that I have kissed Grace Palmer twice." His friends were dumbstruck. He failed to mention that the kissing incidents had taken place a good decade earlier.

At the end of the evening, Grace walked home with her girlfriends. She hadn't danced, not even when Mr. Most Athletic, Floyd Small, asked her to do the Four-step. The sassafras punch courted her until the dance was over. Ben hadn't betrayed her; it was just a reworking of the truth. But Grace knew about the curse of secrets revealed. Once they are inside-out, they can't hide from notice. And the shape of them shifts with the ebb and flow of the witnesses.

The broken mirror was already bringing them bad luck. The trou-ble with Marrow, as Granny Ma'am would often say, was that it was wedded to itself, breeding misfortune and heartache.

Kept by the Lord

Even though Cane was shielded by the black-lace veil, the light of day caused her to raise her hand over her head, palm facing outward, as if she were being attacked. She left the sanctuary so they couldn't stare at her anymore. The visiting minister's words numbed her. For if her face were marked, marked for mercy, what had she done to deserve God's mercy? Sweat glued the veil to her face. The salt from her tears stung the remaining scabs on her face. She tried to breathe in the piercing air of December, she longed for the way it cleared her lungs, but her nostrils were swollen. She only smelled herself or nothing.

Cane passed the homes of her Marrow neighbors. The Haydons, Betsey Sunn, the Ladders, Mitty Hyde, and the Rayfords. If she had felt stronger, she would have walked to Winkie's house, but it was downtown above his father's shop. She would have walked right into his living room, asked him if she could speak to him. If she could, she would have ambled through town with him holding her hand, around the crumbling stone soldier sinking into the earth. She would have held Winkie's hand over her stomach until he felt the flutter, the quick kicks that were keeping her awake most nights.

Instead, she walked heavy heeled along the road to the Lyons' estate. The road was empty and unfamiliar, though she had walked it many times. In spring and summer, the trees, shrubs, and grasses all touched each other. She had not noticed before how vacant nature looked at this time of the year, how things were more separated from one another. She saw Jack

Pliney working in the Lyon's yard. He was one of the few people she knew who lived truthfully. On Sunday, so many people remained indoors until after church, so no one would know they stayed away from a worship service. She'd done it most of her life. Even her mother stayed in until the noon bells rang. But here was Jack Pliney outside honoring, or at least trying to heal, God's earth.

He stopped pruning a wisteria branch and tipped his hat in her direction. Since he'd teased her about Winkie that day at Miss Dunnet's funeral and she'd given him the photography lesson, they had become better acquainted. They mostly had conversations at night or early morning, when he did some of his land-tinkering, and Cane was dipping her feet in the Tear or bringing flowers and songs to the babies' graves at His Glory. As her body grew she didn't hide it from him. He seemed to know everything anyway. She did make a point of telling him one night that she wasn't collecting objects any longer, and he seemed relieved, though not for himself or the Indians he was related to. "It'll be good for your spirit, Cane," he'd said. Cane thought it was the changes in her body that caused her to be more honest.

Cane and her mother lived on the far side of the Lyon property. Their two-story wooden house was trimmed in white and painted China red. Grandma Winnie had grown up there and left the house and surrounding land to Darleen. But it never felt like a family home to Cane. She was sure it belonged to some other family that was going to be showing up any day now.

Her shoes thudded on the stone path and when her foot landed on the porch steps she heard a hissing sound as if the wood could no longer carry her weight. Cane hadn't figured out what to do about the birth of her child. Each day she got bigger, she seemed less able to discuss the matter with her mother. And her mother hardly looked at her face or figure. Somewhere deep down, Cane imagined, the thought, the idea that Cane was with child had occurred to Darleen, but only in the context that it would never happen.

The screen door was locked along with the front door, so she had to wait. A madman who had escaped from the mental institution in Durham was loose in Marrow County and had been sneaking into homes in the area. He was so light on his feet that he'd usually have a good meal or two before anyone noticed, then he'd scamper away like a field mouse at the first sign of another human. Cane's mother couldn't bear the thought of a crazy man in her kitchen, so she started keeping the front door and the screen door locked.

"Mother, open up. It's me," Cane said. She could hear her mother in the kitchen getting Sunday dinner ready. Darleen Walker rarely cooked during the week, but on Sundays she cooked up a big meal. She'd set a complete table for three, although no one but she and Cane would sit down together.

"What brings you back early?" Darleen said. Cane's eyes jeweled with tears as she stepped into the house. "Well, did the Lord get your tongue or what?"

"What did I do? What did I do when I was younger that made God mark me?" Cane could hardly utter the question. Usually on Sundays her mother was in the best of moods and would on occasion reveal some tidbit of Cane's past or her own.

"Lord, Cane. What has that Northerner put into your head?" Darleen said, but there was an inch of concern creasing her forehead.

"Every Sunday you set the table for three people and nobody comes. Who are we? I know the Southern Soldier is a lie; I know who my father is. I know him better than you would think," Cane said. She removed the wet veil and her accommodating coat. A loose sweater underneath concealed her belly. But the salt and sweat from her body had mixed with the black dye of the material and left streaks of gray across her face like veins in a chunk of marble. "Who are you expecting?"

"Now don't get yourself into a fit. You did the same thing when you were little." Darleen went to the kitchen sink and wet a towel. She walked into the dining room and Cane followed her. "So you know who your father is, do you?" She handed Cane the towel. "Well, you're good at digging and snooping, so I guess you would figure it out at some point." She sat down and waved her hand toward Cane.

"This place across from me I set each Sunday is for your father, Buckford Kent, as you already know. It seemed the only way I could keep his memory alive. He gave me this china. We picked it out together at Belks. His folks didn't like me, and I didn't care for them either. They were big furniture people here in the area, and the idea of their son courting a mortician didn't sit well with them one minute. It bothered them that I didn't have rich blood and that I liked my work." Darleen stopped and served herself a large portion of everything: fried chicken, two helpings of butterbeans, pickled beets, cheese potatoes, and three criss-cross rolls. "Also, his folks thought I was an old hen. They were successful at keeping us from marrying. His friends said he died of a broken heart; I just think he died natural, but he did love me." On Sundays, Darleen ate up for the week or for the rest of the family.

"Your Grandma Winnie sent me to her father's farm until you were born. Not that anyone here was surprised, but we hid that kind of thing." Cane served herself a larger portion than her mother's, but her mother didn't notice. "My mother was real good about me being in a family way, except that after every meal she'd make me burn the leftovers on my plate and wash my dishes separate. That was some old superstition her mother had passed down." Darleen piled a spoonful of butterbeans into her mouth and reached across the table for the sweet pickles. Cane thought for a moment she could tell her mother. It would be fine. She, of all people, would understand.

"Did I ever tell you about how Grandma Winnie met Grandpa?" Cane shook her head, more in disbelief about where the conversation had meandered. But her mother revealed their family past in scraps and trims; Cane let her talk because she might otherwise never get a chance to hear this part of her history.

"It was the strangest courtship. Mama lived up by Salem, and when her parents thought she was ready to court men, they just put a candle in the window to let the menfolk know she was ready for bundling. You know about that, when they let the young people sleep side by side in their clothes and in a sleep sack to separate any kind of, well, trouble? Your grandfather was passing through town and needed a place to rest for the night. Imagine how lucky he was. Grandma didn't know him from Adam, but he bundled all week and by Sunday they were in the church getting hitched."

Cane thought the whole bundling idea was a waste of passion and not worth the time of day. The idea of bundling with Winkie appealed to her, though, except that by most standards, they had already crossed the line you never did when bundling.

Darleen looked at Cane like her thoughts had interrupted her mother.

"Grandma said it was his sweet-pickle breath that got her. He'd worked at a packing plant all summer and couldn't get the pickle smell out of him. I think she choked on those watermelon rind pickles just to be next to him again."

"But Mama," Cane said, not sure where the conversation should go at this point. Her mind was full of so many questions and divergent thoughts, she couldn't finish what she had started to say.

"Now what is this talk about mercy and marks? I tell you, just let one of those big-city folks come down here and they turn everyone upside down with their fancy talk." Darleen's mouth was full up and she shook her head in appreciation of herself. She relished her own cooking. "You know, I went to school, too. I had to for my mortician's license."

"What's in my past, Mama?" Cane had not lifted her fork to her mouth, though she was aching with hunger. The child was kicking on both sides as if running a race.

"Well, there's nothing you did, Cane."

"What, Mama? What are you talking about?" Cane put the fork down and wrapped her hands under her belly in a prayer weave.

"That trouble with Riley Trunk is my fault. He liked me something sinful and he was full married. But people talk and there was some chatter that you were ..."

Darleen stopped. Though it was her nature to finish every sentence, she ended this one early. It was one of the only times Cane could recall that her mother thought about her daughter before she spoke.

Cane rocked herself back and forth until she heard one leg of the chair cracked. She looked at her mother. Cane was long done with Riley Trunk.

"See what happens when people out of the area stick their nose in business and stir things up they know nothing about?" Darleen glanced at the empty table settings.

Cane made herself lift her fork up to her mouth. She looked across the table to the place set opposite from hers and wondered how her life would have turned out if her father were sitting there. Would he care about her face?

"Riley Trunk is dead and I say, good riddance!"

Her mother finally got up and went to her room upstairs. Cane stayed in her seat at the table, where her chair and her place were set for her. She heard her mother singing. The words were ones her mother had whispered to herself before she went to sleep when Cane was little.

It's what did you have for supper, Bucky boy, my only one?
Oh, what did you have for supper, my — own sweet one?
Sweet milk and sweet parsnips.
My dear, make the bed soon.
For I'm tired at the heart and I want to lie down.
Bucky, my only one.

Cane kept brushing her hands over her stomach. *Mama didn't want to know.* Cane tried to keep her mind off the vacant seat across from her. At least she knew that truth. Just as Cane was pushing herself away from the table, her mother returned to the room.

"Here. You can have this. I guess you'll be wanting to know what he looked like." Darleen handed Cane a picture of a man standing by the soldier in the square. He was old, sickly looking, with a curly mustache like she'd seen in the silent movies. She saw his jawbone, and saw herself in his chin and cheeks. Her finger outlined his body. So, all these years the lullaby Cane had heard and wondered about was a love song from her mother to her father. Cane realized that her mother's singing had been of her loss and sorrow. Darleen had loved this odd man Cane never would know, so Cane had to piece together the meaning and believe there was one for her to carry on.

Circling Winter

"In this town, everything is like a chemistry experiment just about to explode in your face," one of Winkie Jr.'s chums said to a familiar group that had gathered outside Winkie's father's shop. Winkie had been away in Florida, so he came around to catch up and show off.

"Cane Walker's an experiment that already did," the boy added, squishing his face together with both hands.

Winkie Jr.'s eyes stopped twitching, though none of his friends picked up on this. "Your father must be tuckered out these days," Winkie Jr. said to the boy who didn't know yet how sorry he would be for the remark about Cane. "I hear you'll be a big brother soon, though I guess if I were to be accurate, I'd have to say half-brother, and I don't think your mama stirred up the trouble." The boy looked to all his friends and then fell silent, his eyes staring at no one in particular as surprise, anger, and then tears on the verge of falling passed by his visual path, before the boy caught himself and snorted them back into the depths of his mind.

Winkie stepped backward after he heard himself deliver his response, as if the force of his own words had shoved him in reverse. He'd never cut someone to the core so deeply and with such speed. He knew the truth from his father, yet he knew too much truth about a lot of people in town. But there was no need to pass it along. There were plenty of people in Marrow who did that as a matter of duty. Duty to whom, Winkie could never figure out. God maybe. Eye for an eye, and he had just taken one from a childhood friend. He pondered about the meanness, if it was a by-product of being in love. In love with Cane, he thought. He felt randomly territorial like a lion or more like a rabid dog.

"You been away for a spell, Winkie," another boy said after they all couldn't stand the silence a split second longer. "I bet you headed to Sparks for some fun, eh?"

The six boys were gun-eyed in anticipation of Winkie's answer. Winkie Jr.'s eyes blinked as if the motion ticked off the thoughts in his mind. She can't stay. Blink. Where would she go? Blink. There is no one to tell.

"I started toward Sparks and ended up with my mother's relatives in Florida. I just showed up and they were happier than Jesus to see me. Had my fill of rattlesnake, I kid you not." Even the boy Winkie Jr. had embarrassed looked up. "I ate alligator steaks, too. Went out in the swamps with my cousin and shot one right between the eyes. He was dead-eyed to death. His beady balls stayed open like we'd scared the living daylights out of him. And we had." The truth will keep your eyes open, Winkie said to himself.

"My father says you must be courting the devil to eat rattlesnake. I'd kill it, but I'd never swallow it," remarked one of his friends. The rest scoffed at the comment. The dry clay at their feet was easily kicked into a dust that peppered their bodies. Winkie pawed at a clump of clay that didn't give. His father's shop was full of old timers. It was soda time, late afternoon when work ended, though for some work had ceased long ago. He kicked some of the clay into the side of the brick building. His friends followed suit. What Winkie was intending to do he did not know; what happened next was that the boys started kicking clay so powerfully that one shoe, whose it was didn't really matter, kicked a large, heavy chunk straight into Winkie Sr.'s window. It shattered slowly, the way creeping heat spreads. The boys stopped and watched the shards fall to the ground and land in a pattern that could have been said to be artistic.

"Boy, now we've done it." The group of boys said as one. There was no use running since they were in plain view of the nosiest people in town.

Some of the money he'd saved for the baby would now have to be used to replace the window.

Winkie Sr. and all the patrons ran outside to inspect the commotion. It was bad enough that Winkie's father had been inside. But many of the other boys' fathers had been inside as well. A collective weight of disappointment pushed the boys to lower their heads, even as they resisted.

"What is the matter with you boys? Y'all are old enough to have families and you act like hoodlums," Winkie Sr. said to the whole group, but his eyes lingered on his son, as if he'd just realized his son was indeed a grownup. "I've a mind to send y'all out to the wilds of Alaska and set your fate." Without saying a word, Winkie Jr. went inside the shop, brought out three brooms and handed them out to his friends.

Winkie Jr. could see his mother looking down from the upstairs window. The look on her face was one, Winkie Jr. guessed, of distraught disbelief. He had no idea whether she had observed the whole incident. There would be a small article about it in the *Daily Gazette*. Winkie smiled at the thought. He blew a tiny kiss to his mother not out of disrespect but as a farewell. As if divinely informed, she waved back at him. Though his father had fumed about his sudden trip to Florida, his mother had been quietly pleased. Her relatives never visited Marrow. She shut the curtains. Her hands remained in a prayer position with the two lace panels between them for a good minute.

"If I hurry, Father, I can get the replacement glass at Mr. Adams' out Highway 40." Winkie noticed he didn't apologize, even though he had meant to. His father studied him, came close enough to brush the red dust off Winkie Jr.'s chin.

"I need to go out that way myself. I'll get it." Winkie Jr.

knew that his father had a prearranged meeting with the river thieves.

"When you finish cleaning up this mess. I need you to mind the store, ya hear?"

"If you ask me," one of his customers said, "I think he's lost his mind. I don't think he'll find it in your shop."

Everyone laughed, except Winkie Jr., Winkie Sr., and the embarrassed boy who had just caught the eye of his father.

Bound to Mercy
(Mercy)

I've been home for the holidays since the second week of December. After getting a scholarship at 16 to the nursing school in Greensboro, I thought I'd be able to stay away from town for a while. They let me enroll early because I was so good in health science and math. I lied to them a bit and said my father was sick and I needed to become a nurse as soon as possible. But the school closed for vacation over Christmas and New Year's, just like high school.

For ages, Lily and I had heard the rumors of my mother and Ben Ladder. First, it was the affair and then as I grew up I heard more. A neighbor told me about the way my mother and Ben would go to the bathroom at the same time so they could send some coded message through their windows. Like Nella and Minish, Mother and Ben had their own secret language. Neighbors often tell you things that sear you.

This Christmas Eve, Lily and I decided to head over to His Glory Cemetery where, we now suspected, Mama and Ben always met for a holiday tumble in one of the mausoleums. This year Ben wasn't doing too well, his own burden of guilt about busted him in half. Some people struggle and move on with their living, but Ben Ladder was stuck in the middle, going nowhere. His brother had been trapped in a foxhole during the war and lived to tell it, but Ben Ladder was stuck in a chicken hole to this day. He couldn't be with my mother, and he wasn't the kind of man to leave his wife. I had heard the minister whisper to Mitty Hyde at Winkie Sr.'s Soda Shop that

Ben fell from Grace because of Grace. But no one else talked about them anymore; there was too much other stuff happening in town and in the rest of the world. Who cared anyway? Daddy seemed immune to it. My mother just kept on living like she always did. Still no mirrors in the house. We weren't sure they would meet, but Daddy had gone off as usual and Mama had started cooking up a hurricane of holiday delights.

Being in nursing school had taught me about what was never said in my family or town. Bodies are like land, and you need to take care of them, or else they will rot and go to weed. I've been corresponding with Mr. Pliney about the conditions of the soil in and around town. He's convinced there is poison in the dirt and it bleeds into the plants where it is eaten by the livestock, and has seeped into the wells. The death rate in our county is higher than most. For years, Mr. Pliney has been carefully growing vegetables and fruit in his small plot of land that Mr. Lyon gave him after he cured the apple trees. He uses fertilizers made from herbs and roots and never lets any kind of chemical contaminate his acreage. Some at Tillie's Grocery & Feed think he is on the far side of insane. His daughter moved out west a long time ago. Actually, he sent her to a cousin of his because he wanted her away from the evil that sifts in and out of the earth in this part of the country.

Sent his daughter away. My father would never do that to me. Never. Sent his daughter away. Maybe Mr. Pliney is just a crazy Negro after all.

Lily and I made sure we got to the cemetery in plenty of time. We dressed in black and veiled ourselves so we could pretend we were mourning a recently deceased member of our community. There are always extra deaths around the holidays in Marrow, so we knew we'd be able to find a mound of fresh dirt. And since it was Christmastime we could pretend we were visiting kin and no one would care.

We waited like diligent children in the act of an important

deed or adventure. We planned to confront them and make them repent, or that was my plan. I think Lily just wanted to see for herself if there was any truth to the rumors.

About 5 p.m., as the winter light faded behind the Lyon Mausoleum, we saw Mr. Pliney show up with Cane Walker. She was crying and holding onto her belly. Lily looked at me for guidance. She was still pretty young in the ways of the world. Cane was a good seven, maybe eight months gone. No one took the time of day to look at her, since they were all scared of the bumpy mask of skin covering her brain and skull. I don't know why folks veered away from her so much. I'd seen worse in the emergency room. Her baggy working jacket hid a lot. I guess no one in town suspected, yet Ulla Trunk had once told me she saw her daddy grab at Cane one evening in the cotton fields, but that was a long while back, and Ulla was sure it wasn't an ongoing relationship.

Lily and I heard Cane cry out, "There's blood." She and Mr. Pliney stepped up to the Lyon Mausoleum with a key that Mr. Pliney removed from underneath a marble vase by the iron gate.

"There's going to be blood, Cane. Steady yourself."

He held two blankets in one hand while he led her through the wooden door with the other. Lily tried to follow but I held her back. I knew my mother was yet to arrive. And wouldn't she be surprised at the visitors. As I grabbed my sister and pulled her to her knees above the new grave, I heard my mother approach. She was walking with Ben Ladder like they were best friends or a couple, which I guess they were. Both. But they did not look like they were there for each other. They spoke in normal tones and hurried not out of lust, it seemed to me, but because other matters crossed their minds. My mother carried a basket with steam drifting out of it. "There they are!" Lily said, loud enough that they turned in our direction but bowed their heads in deference to our dead. Lily was nine and still in awe of adventure. She was the honest one in the family, yet she was somehow the one who never figured out what was really true. She never knew much about the baby boy. Just hearsay. Lily seemed to be protected by her ability to be so forthcoming, it took up all the room in a conversation and left her satisfied and content but none the wiser.

We moved a little closer and heard Cane screaming. As curious as Lily was, the female noise from Cane made her pause.

"Mercy, we shouldn't be here. We were not invited."

"Go home if you want and be ignorant the rest of your days."

With a challenge like that even Lily decided to remain. We got to the iron gate and saw a trail of blood like snail markings. There was the jolting smell of winter in the air and the echoing sounds of a cemetery that was being disturbed when it was usually ignored.

I heard Mr. Pliney say to my mother and Ben, "We need a doctor, there is too much blood too soon."

It was Lily who pushed me forward. She didn't know all the layers between our mother and Ben and maybe that is why I held my ground and forgot my nurse's creed. She shoved me again with the same rage I had often shoved her with when we were younger.

Inside Cane lay on the floor, though Mr. Pliney had put the blankets beneath her. My mother had brought strips of rags and hot water. Ben was washing Cane's forehead like she was his own. The room was lit with candles of mixed sizes, and it smelled of sacks of molded fruit and old tobacco. When they turned to us as we entered, no one said a word, except Cane."Mercy," she said as her lips bit down on the pain, "save my baby."

And though I wanted to go back to school, out of this town, I was now bound by my ability to help her. My mother and

Ben moved aside for me. Lily crouched in the corner. She was too stunned to notice my mother and Ben's names scratched into the blue marble. No one liked looking at Cane Walker's face, and with this kind of pain and anguish, it was hard not to run at the sight of her. I had to steady my hands and forget who Cane was. She was just another patient like they reminded us in the hospital school every day.

Bits and pieces of the child started to come out. My mother and Ben were unable to help me. Mr. Pliney had lost his wife in childbirth many years before, yet he assisted me, though I heard him whisper, "Oh, Celie." In the past few years he and Cane had become friends, like outsiders do, so he felt compelled to follow this thing to the end.

I knew the child was dead. I had known earlier by the way the blood rushed out of her, like the Tear River in spring.

But her body was not done. It kept shooting out parts of the baby's anatomy. It was a girl. When a tiny hand floating in blood and amniotic fluid fell palm up on the blanket, even Mr. Pliney broke down and cried. Lily yelped for Mama, and Ben held the two of them or they held him. I didn't expect much courage from anyone. Those fifteen red recordings wouldn't help me here either.

Cane's words were rough like the rocks in a drybed. She gulped candle air. "Why not for me?" she called out and the words echoed in the mausoleum like a chorus. But no one answered back.

"Is the face all right?" she asked coming out of the grief for a second. I had been curious about the face too and had noted how perfect it was as it emerged.

"Yes," Pliney and I answered in unison. I dipped the rags in water and carefully washed her clean of it. And I looked over at my mother and knew at that moment she wasn't thinking of Cane. There was the blue boy again between us. Miles was his name. And I think she named me Mercy as much for him as for me. I heard Lily say to Mama and Ben, "Sorry about the baby. I planted the seeds for you both but nothing grew." And there was Lily talking like that at a time like this.

In school they taught us to see each emergency as a series of facts. Life. Death. Follow procedures. Keep the emotions away from your work. Mr. Pliney and I put the baby's remains in the basket that my mother had brought. Lily came over to Cane and held her hand. We all surrounded her and everyone else wept.

The next day, Cane, Winkie Jr., Mr. Pliney, my mother, Ben, Lily, and I met at the cemetery so early that the morning light of Christmas hadn't quite arrived. Winkie Jr. of all people was the father. We gathered for the funeral of Cane's child, whom she had named Mary. Darleen, none the wiser, was absent. Winkie Jr. stood next to Cane and he was holding her hand so tightly their hands looked stuck to each other. He tried without success to keep his own tears from falling. In the rising light they looked like a couple, like a couple that belonged to each other. The marks on Cane's face were well defined from crying so hard. Nearby, I heard the snowbirds making their kissy sound.

Cane had decided she wanted the remains to go into her father's grave. "I had a father, I have his jawline," she said to all of us, and we nodded our heads, though no one knew the truth one way or the other. Cane and Mr. Pliney dug up the coffin and opened it with ease. Along with the child, Cane had an open sack stuffed with items that she placed into the decaying box.

Lily told me later she was close enough to see some of them. A gold-and-black pin; a pocketknife; a gem-studded picture frame with a photo of Cane, Winkie, and the basket-baby; and a number of teeth.

Before Cane let go of the sack she looked in my direction and pulled out a paper from the inside.

We were frozen, not by the chill of morning — it was an unseasonably warm Christmas day — but by the emptiness in our hearts that had filled with despair and left our bodies shivering. Cane patted at a locket around her neck and slowly pulled it off and laid it with the other things. The blue barrette that had kept her brown hair out of her sad eyes shimmered and marked her with sunlight.

As the coffin was returned to its resting spot, there was silence amid our small crowd of mourners. The men covered it with dirt. Cane put moss all over the fresh grave. Winkie placed a blue violet on top of the green covering. No one had the right words. We were all tongue-tied.

When we left the cemetery, Cane handed me a letter. The letter of my past. I knew it was just for my eyes to see; I didn't unfold it until I was back at school.

Of course, I didn't know it wouldn't be addressed to me.

Dear Miles,

It's not much I know to write you now. Now that you rest some-where else. I once felt your heartbeat like wheat tapping at the wind. That swift kick you made at odd hours of the day kept your mother up. She'd arrive at church sleepy-eyed, turning away from me as usual. You were a secret gift just between us and the Lord.

After I heard the news, I called the head nurse in the maternity ward at the hospital. I told her I was a reporter doing research on dif-ficult births in Marrow County. I asked her about you. She was hesi-tant to speak, as if her words would still harm you or herself. She said you came out blue, like the egg of a woodthrush, you were all puffed up, lethargic, like you'd drowned in your own womb water.

I didn't answer her right away. I was trembling. She told me more than I thought I wanted to hear. Silence does that. It makes others speak their private voice. She said your mother kept calling for someone who wasn't in the waiting room.

I need to pass through this valley of grief about you. But I wear you, Miles, with me always like a crest.

I would have rocked you in my arms and let my tears wash the death-color away. I would have.

Your mother cannot be near me. I like to think it is her desire for me that keeps her distant.

I love her more as the hours pass. The curve of her arm. The way the sunlight falls through the strands of her hair at dusk.

The faith that we will all be a family one day keeps me sane.

With love.

Your Father,

Benjamin Ladder

I carry this letter with me, as I try to decipher what names and love really should mean.

Town Gossip
(Betsey Sunn Speaks Again)

No one knows exactly what happened to Riley Trunk. Some think the Skeeter Grove boys came onto his property and shot him, while they were stealing a batch of watermelons, and dumped him in the Tear. Others are sure it was the river thieves having a good day of raising a ruckus and Riley Trunk just got in their way. Ina Ladder thinks the ghost of Rachel Trunk came back and rung him out for all his sins against his family, and then tossed him into an unforgiving current. When the sheriff went by to check up on the Trunk property, he found that wild grapes had taken over his other crops. There were no other signs of disturbance except the pigs had somehow gotten inside the house, and, well, you can imagine the stench.

The only thing of significance they found from Riley Trunk's body in Wrightsville was an old high-school picture of Darleen Walker in his pocket. They traced it to Marrow because it had The Best Photographs in Town, Marrow, NC, stamped on the back. All that did was to set everyone wondering if Cane was Riley's child. But no one would wish that legacy on her. There was so much talk about the Riley Trunk trouble, only a select few were focused enough on Cane and knew she had other worries. Darleen Walker made a point of going to Tillie's Grocery & Feed and to Winkie Sr.'s Soda Shop to flat out deny the evil insinuation. Said she was going to get herself a Philadelphia lawyer to set everyone straight.

Those of us who were around back when she was younger believe her because we know she and Buckford Kent walked nightly around that square so often they almost left a groove in the road. But most others haven't taken to Darleen and her way of living. She is a sinner, and not the only one in town; there are others besides Darleen and Riley Trunk. Yes, children and adults have been hurt, carelessly, inadvertently. But didn't that visiting minister tell us all to let go of the sins others have made against us or God? Mark yourself with mercy and follow it up with forgiveness.

If you believed that visiting minister at the Presbyterian Church, you'd think Darleen's mark of mercy was her daughter and she should remember that; but now no one asked me, did they?

They never do.

A Family Portrait before a Family Funeral
December 24, 1958
Marrow, North Carolina

Her small hands didn't shake like one would expect. She got the camera ready. Winkie Jr. hadn't arrived yet. Cane needed a bit more time to set up the shot. Portraits take time and patience, though most people don't understand that. The doctor in Marrow had said to her that the best photographer he ever knew was a man who was a brain surgeon first. Get all your tools in order. Lay them out. Prepare the body. Cut. Cane worked just the same way. She had to set up the shot and would hold onto the self-portrait cord so she could take three pictures. Three chances to get it right. Her body ached, like pulled muscles do, like it had been wind beaten, like she was no longer herself but one of her mother's sample urns, heavy and empty. Cane put camphor rags on each breast after letting the material sit in the basket with Mary. Grace Haydon had told her that the odor-filled material and the smell of the baby would draw out some of the milk, and later some of the pain in her chest might ease up.

This was the first time she would photograph herself face on. She would stand next to Winkie like a new bride and smile. The image had to reveal truth and not the set-up, the imitation of life that she created for her customers. And she was a bride, a blood bride. She thought about Mary and hoped that some-where beyond she would be able to hold the sparkling frame and look at her parents. *Sleep baby, sleep.* They would have that carved on her marker. Would Mary know that her mother's face was abnormal? Would her father wink just as the photograph was snapped and look like he was asleep or dead? Cane had put the tarnished locket from the Dunnet baby around her neck. Inside were a few strands of Mary's newborn hair. She would use the glossy wedding paper to print from the negative.

Winkie entered the shop and Cane saw the flapping eyelids, slowed only by tears. He would look alive in the portrait in that way folks do when they have suffered or have been tortured. His eyes sagged and appeared bewildered like he didn't expect his life to run off this way. Jack Pliney and Ben had gone to his house to tell him. She knew in his original avoidance of her as her belly thickened, there was also a triumph that he had made something new. He would want to know and she hoped he would come to her shop.

He hadn't witnessed the messy birth-death; but he knew part of the baby had been washed away. What was left of her was contained in a reed basket.

"She's over there if you want to see her."

Winkie Jr. stepped backward. Cane forgot even at this moment most people couldn't look at dead bodies, especially one in pieces.

"Did it hurt her?" he asked. Cane shook her head. "You?" Winkie reached over to her and linked his ring finger with hers.

The able hands of Mercy Haydon had finished the job her body had started. Nurse Mercy, the wandering Haydon girl.

"Now we need to show Mary how much we wanted her," Cane said. Cane reached over and cradled the basket in her arms. She had wrapped Mary in her grandmother's Marrow plaid and a bit of it hung outside of the basket. Winkie came up next to her and positioned his arm solidly around her waist.

Dressed in their Sunday best they stood next to one another, so close that they could have been connected, so pure of spirit, you might have thought they were new in town. *Click. Click. Click.*

Acknowledgements

Any piece of writing relies on the generosity of family and strangers. In this case, my parents Jane Brooks and Charles Sherwood were quite willing to answer the onslaught of questions I asked them throughout the years. In addition, the stranger who became a mentor and friend, Cristina Garcia, believed in this work from the beginning, when I took her class on novel writing at Mills College in 1998. Scott Brown edited the earliest version of the novel and encouraged me to finish it and told me it was a worthy piece of writing. Along the way there have been a variety of people who helped me get this done and resources that inspired me. I am grateful to the librarians in North Carolina and in the San Francisco Bay Area for their time and diligence. To the Center for Southern Culture in Oxford, Mississippi, for their wealth of information and history on the South. The Frank C. Brown Collection of North Carolina Folklore was an invaluable tool and resource. The clever works of Lord Byron, in particular his poem, "Lines inscribed on a Cup formed from a Skull," enhanced Darleen's character on page 51 and page 52. Paul Tillich's sermon, "You Are Accepted," and Henry Emerson Fosdick's sermon, "Shall the Fundamenalists Win?" expanded my knowledge of religious thought.

In particular I would like to thank Judy Hardin at Slow Morning and a Slow Rain Press for not only inspiring me, but also pushing me to publish and to Judith Adamson, for just assuming the book would get out there. I would like to thank

those who helped me in the last stretch, my 11th hour team
— Michael Rosenthal for his careful and insightful editing,
Alane Bowling for her steady and skilled proofreading, Audrey
Karleskind for her attention to detail and creativity with the
cover design. Additionally, I am indebted to my friends and
family, Cathy Crowe, Katherine Dehart, all my sisters, and in
particular, Priscilla McCoy, who has been the best sister one
could ever ask for and has helped me through the thick and
thin of this project from my MFA thesis to the final product.

A writer makes life very challenging for other members of
the immediate family. I wouldn't have gotten this far without
the quiet support of my better half, Timothy Holton, and our
terrific and talented daughter, EJ.

About the Author

S tephanie McCoy was born in Florida and spent many a summer driving across country to North Carolina to visit relatives after her family moved out West. She currently lives in Northern California. This is her first novel.